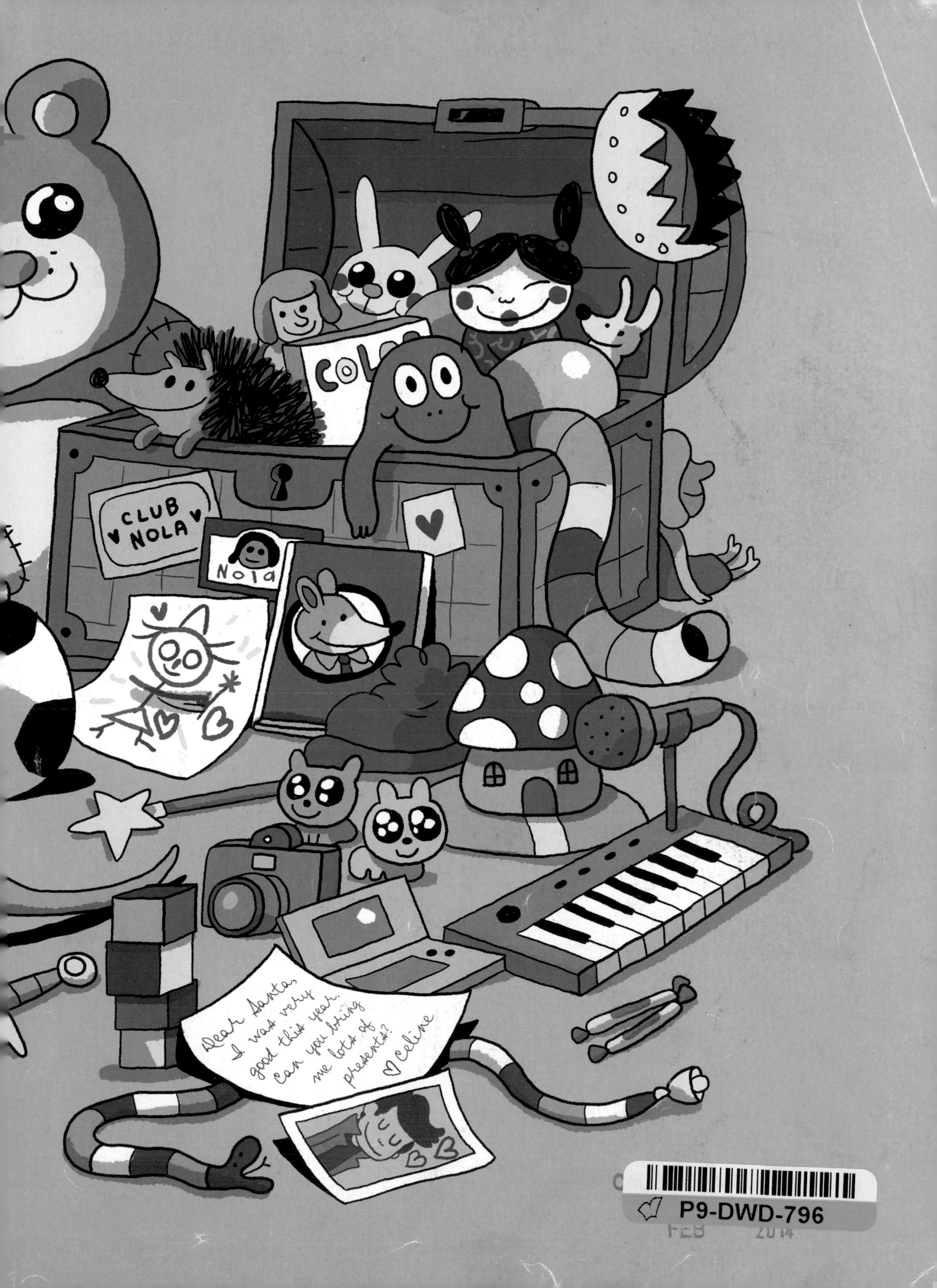
CLUB NOLA
Nola
Dear Santa,
I was very
good this year.
Can you bring
me lots of
presents?
♥Celine

where's Leopold? 2

Snowball Truce!

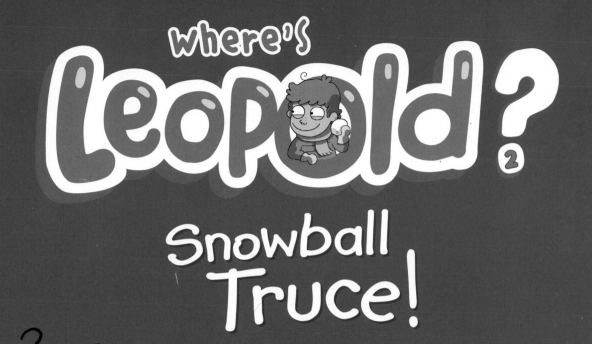

by **Michel-Yves Schmitt**
illustrated by **Vincent Caut**

Graphic Universe™ • Minneapolis • New York

The authors would like to thank Leopold's readers.

Thanks also to Vincent   —Michel-Yves
Thanks also to Michel-Yves   —Vincent

Story by Michel-Yves Schmitt
Art by Vincent Caut
Translation by Carol Klio Burrell

English translation copyright © 2013 by Lerner Publishing Group, Inc.

First American edition published in 2013 by Graphic Universe™.
Published by arrangement with MEDIATOON LICENSING—France.

Où es-tu Léopold?
2/Un pacte en hiver
© DUPUIS 2011—Caut & Schmitt
www.dupuis.com

Graphic Universe™
A division of Lerner Publishing Group, Inc.
241 First Avenue North
Minneapolis, MN 55401 U.S.A.

Website address: www.lernerbooks.com

Library of Congress Cataloging-in-Publication Data

Schmitt, Michel-Yves.
     [Pacte en hiver. English]
     Snowball truce! / by Michel-Yves Schmitt ; illustrated by Vincent Caut ; translation by Carol
Klio Burrell. — 1st American ed.
         p.   cm. — (Where's Leopold? ; #2)
     Summary: Leopold wants to use his invisibility to launch the best snowball fight of all time, but
his older sister, Celine, thinks he should be using his powers for the greater good.
     ISBN 978–1–4677–0770–1 (lib. bdg. : alk. paper)
     ISBN 978–1–4677–1657–4 (eBook)
     1. Graphic novels. [1. Graphic novels. 2. Brothers and sisters—Fiction. 3. Invisibility—
Fiction.] I. Caut, Vincent, ill. II. Burrell, Carol Klio. III. Title.
PZ7.7.S37Sno 2013
741.5'944—dc23   2012042495

Manufactured in the United States of America
1 – MG – 7/15/13

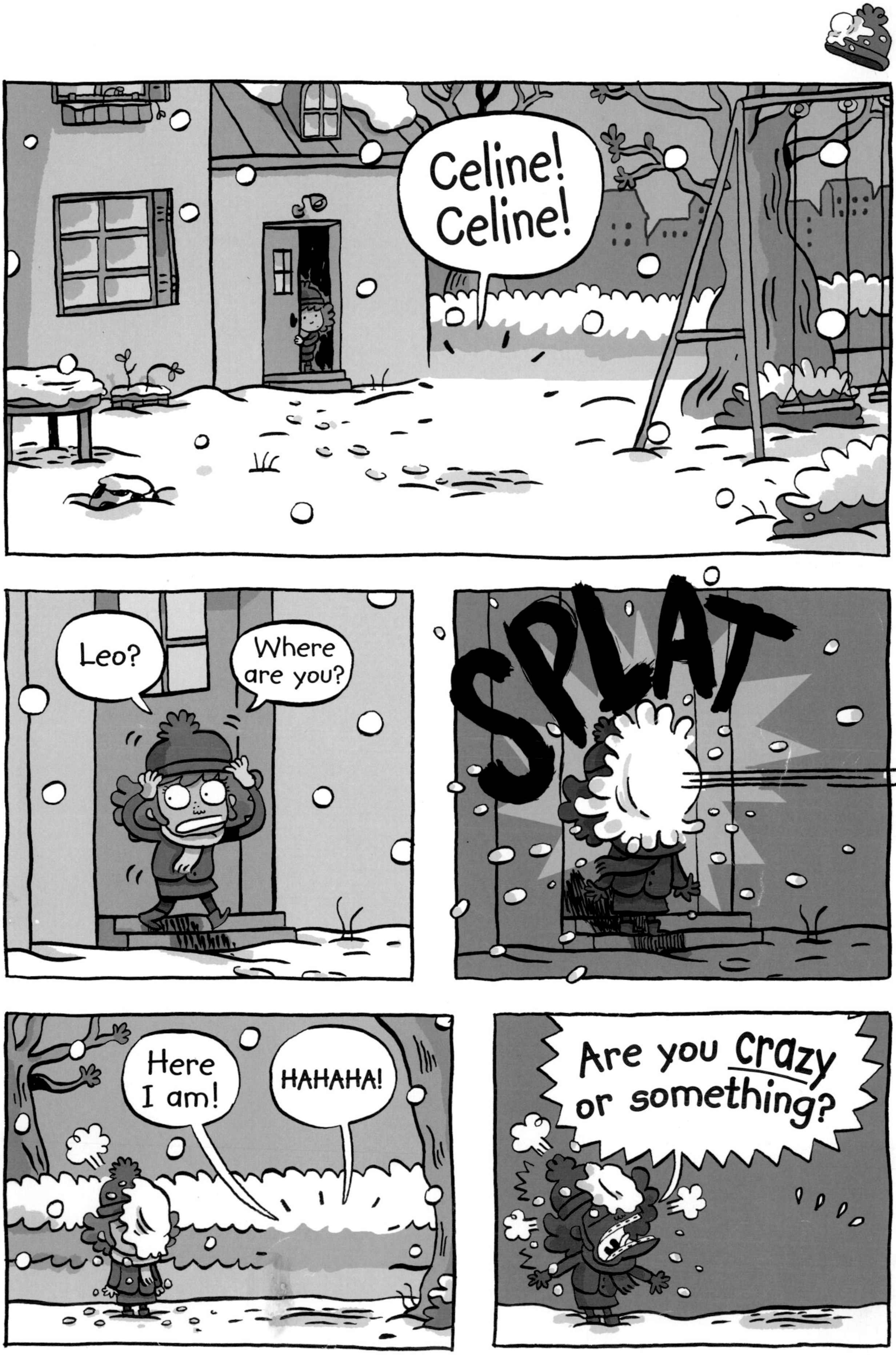
Celine! Celine!
Leo?
Where are you?
SPLAT
Here I am!
HAHAHA!
Are you crazy or something?

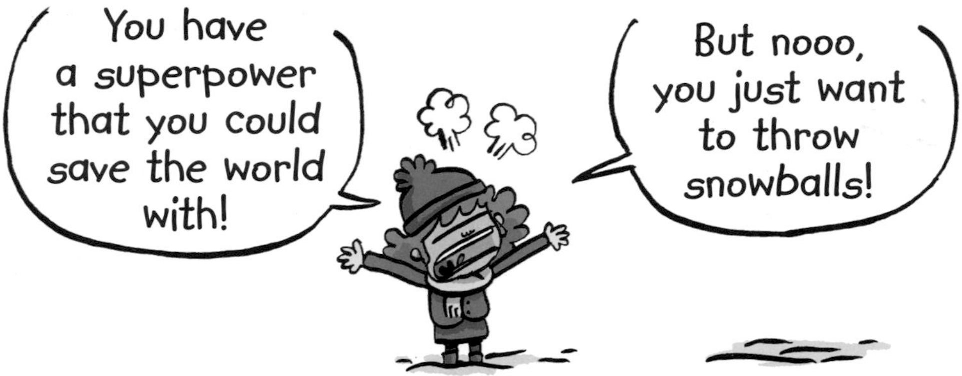
You have a superpower that you could save the world with!
But nooo, you just want to throw snowballs!

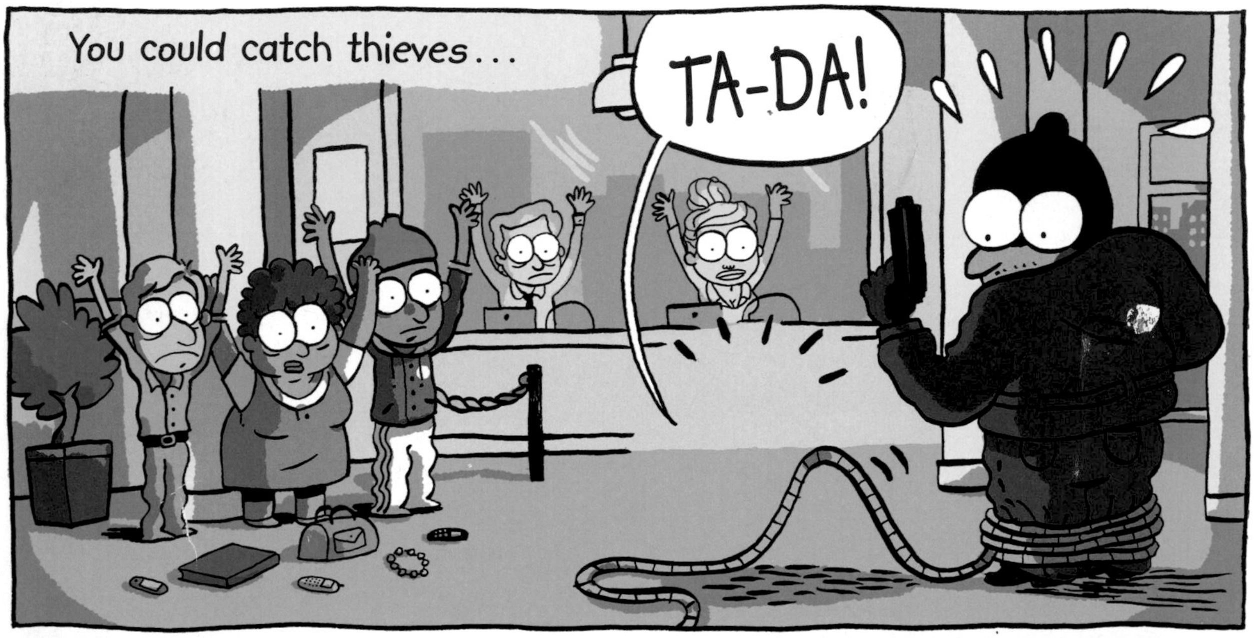
You could catch thieves...
TA-DA!

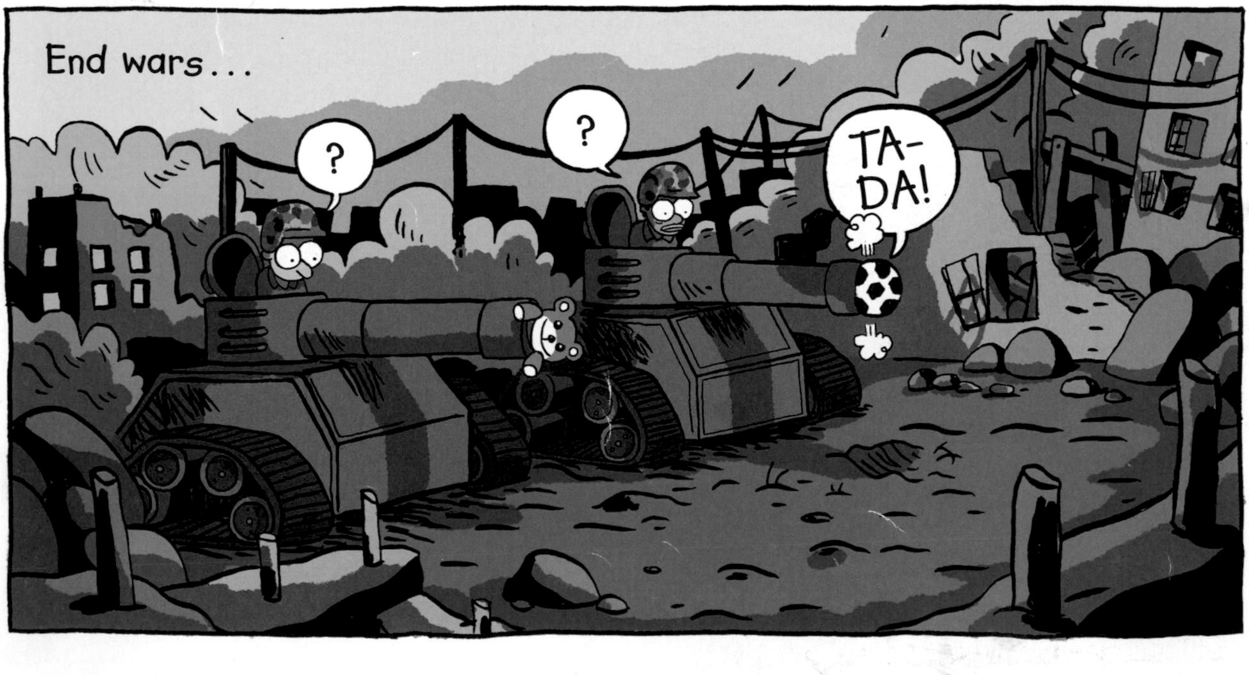
End wars...
?
?
TA-DA!

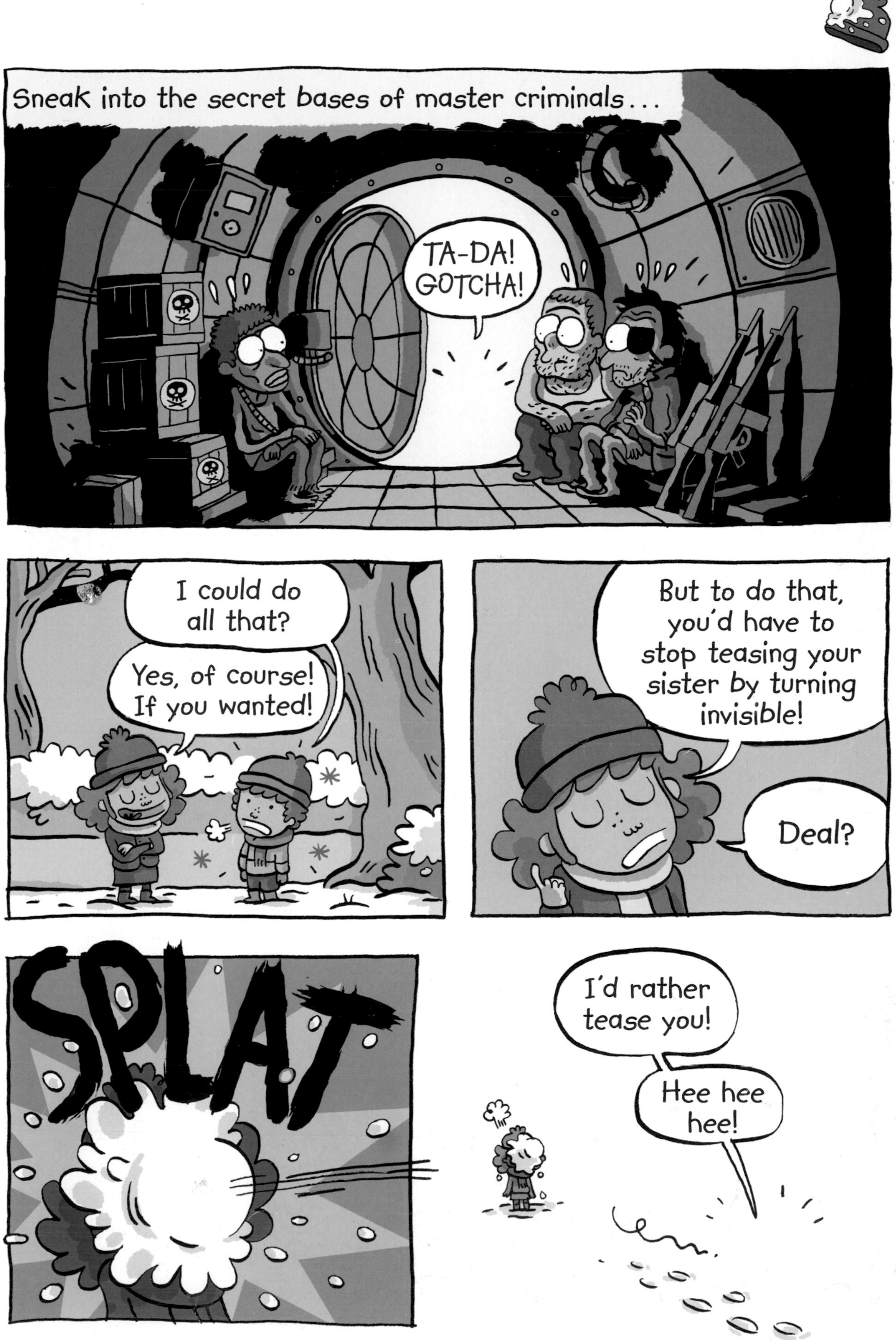
Sneak into the secret bases of master criminals...
TA-DA! GOTCHA!
I could do all that?
Yes, of course! If you wanted!
But to do that, you'd have to stop teasing your sister by turning invisible!
Deal?
SPLAT
I'd rather tease you!
Hee hee hee!

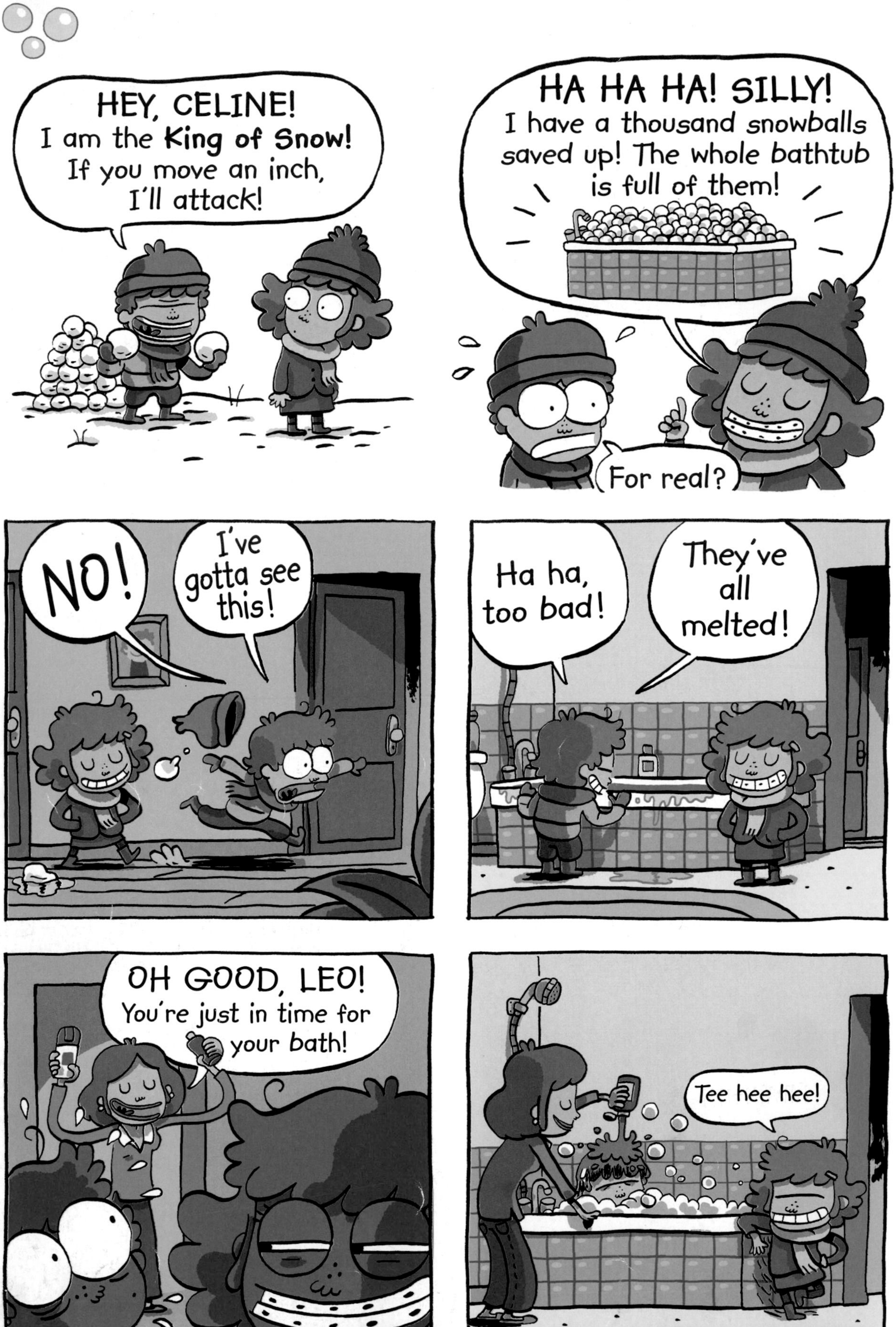

HEY, CELINE! I am the King of Snow! If you move an inch, I'll attack!
HA HA HA! SILLY! I have a thousand snowballs saved up! The whole bathtub is full of them!
For real?
NO!
I've gotta see this!
Ha ha, too bad!
They've all melted!
OH GOOD, LEO! You're just in time for your bath!
Tee hee hee!

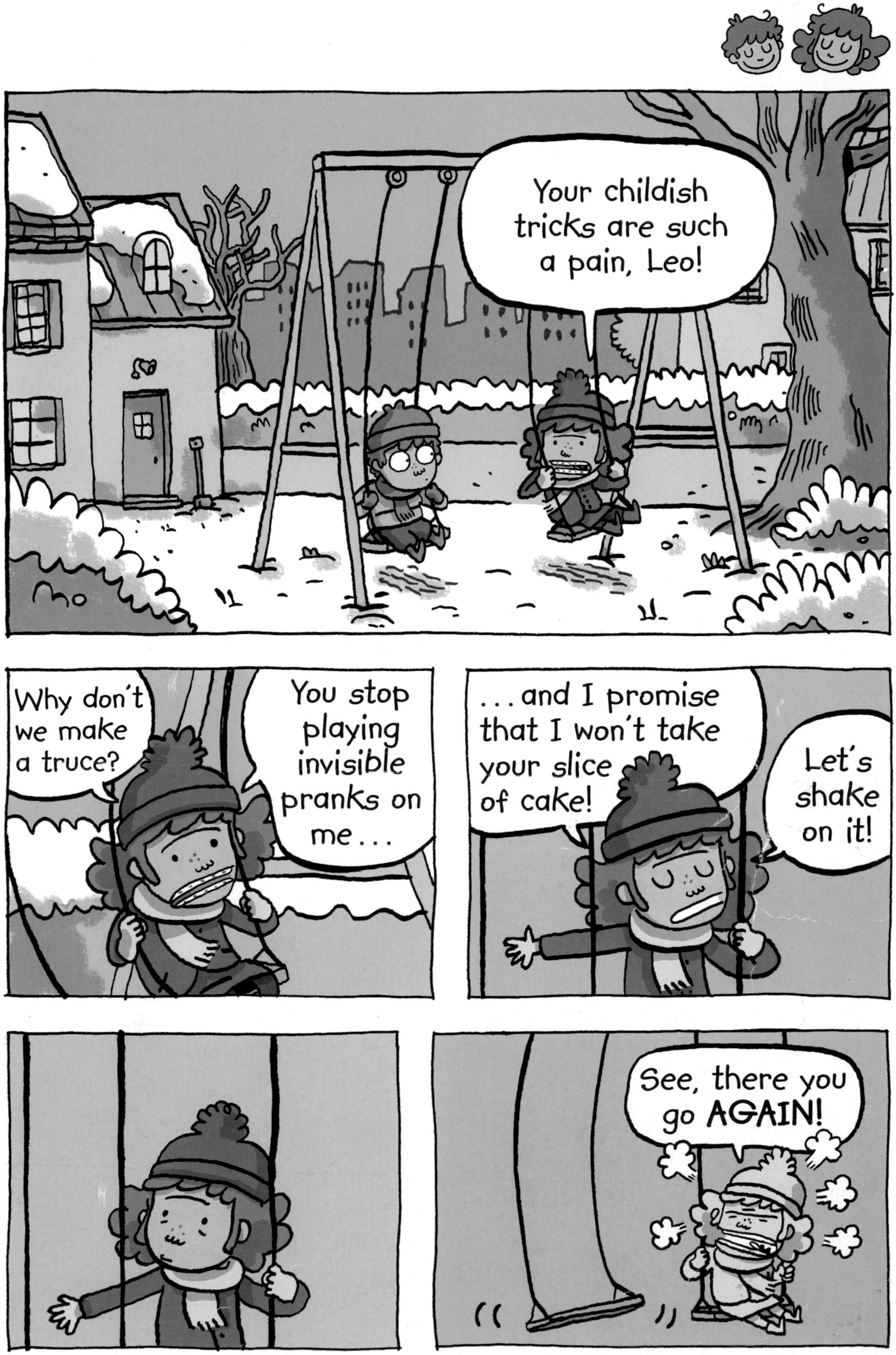

Your childish tricks are such a pain, Leo!
Why don't we make a truce?
You stop playing invisible pranks on me...
...and I promise that I won't take your slice of cake!
Let's shake on it!
See, there you go **AGAIN!**

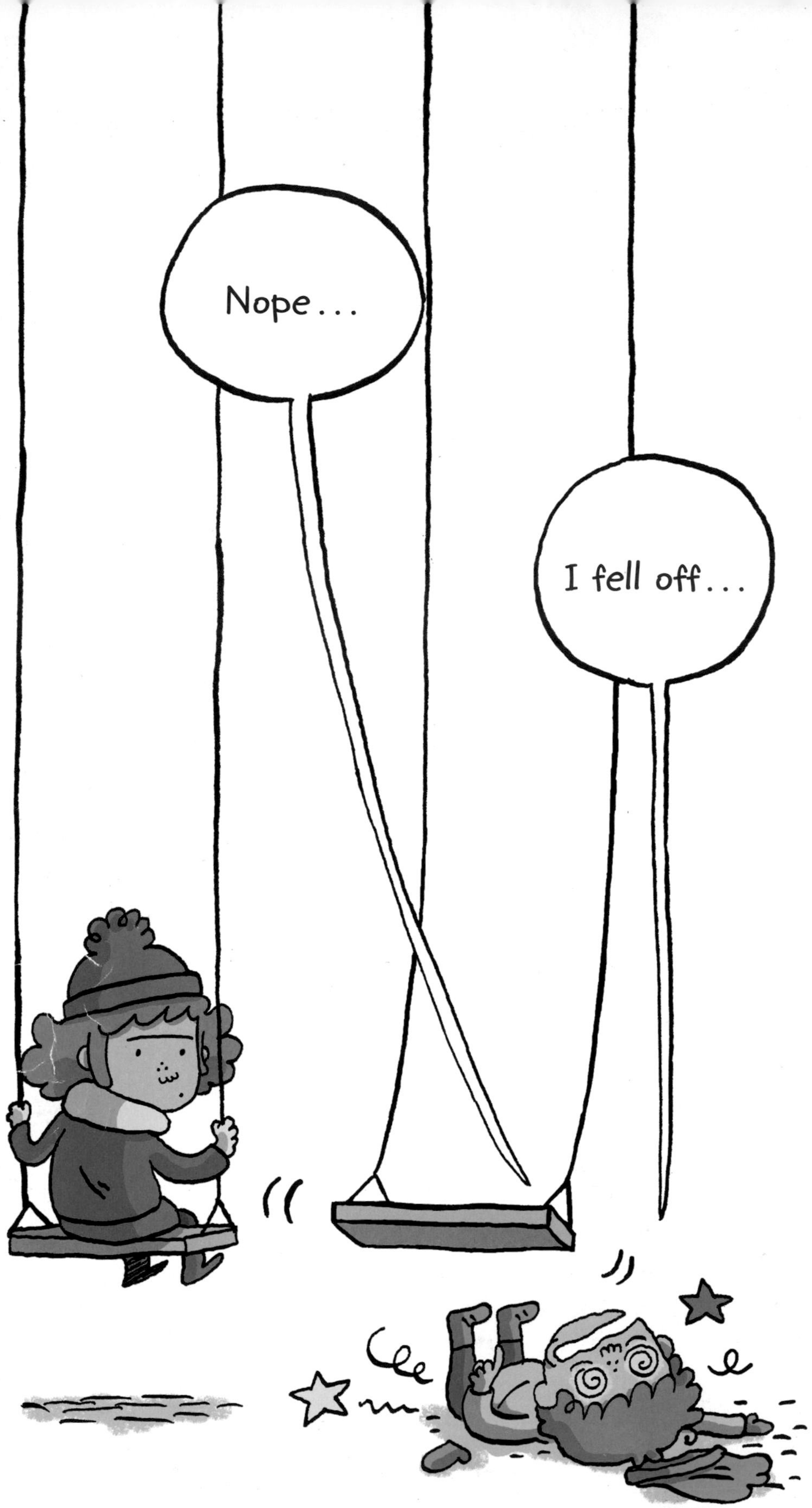
Nope...
I fell off...

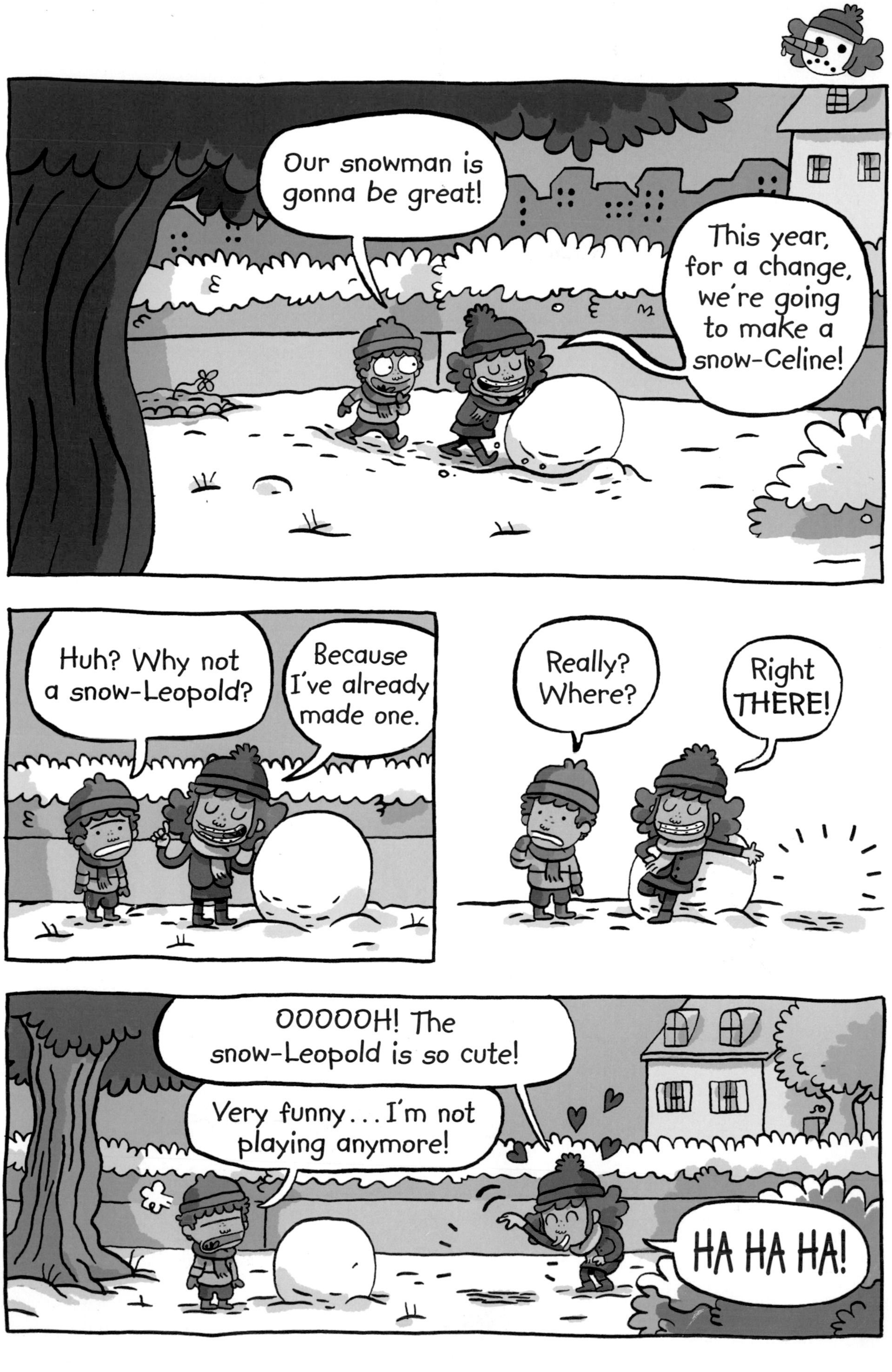
Our snowman is gonna be great!
This year, for a change, we're going to make a snow-Celine!
Huh? Why not a snow-Leopold?
Because I've already made one.
Really? Where?
Right THERE!
OOOOOH! The snow-Leopold is so cute!
Very funny... I'm not playing anymore!
HA HA HA!

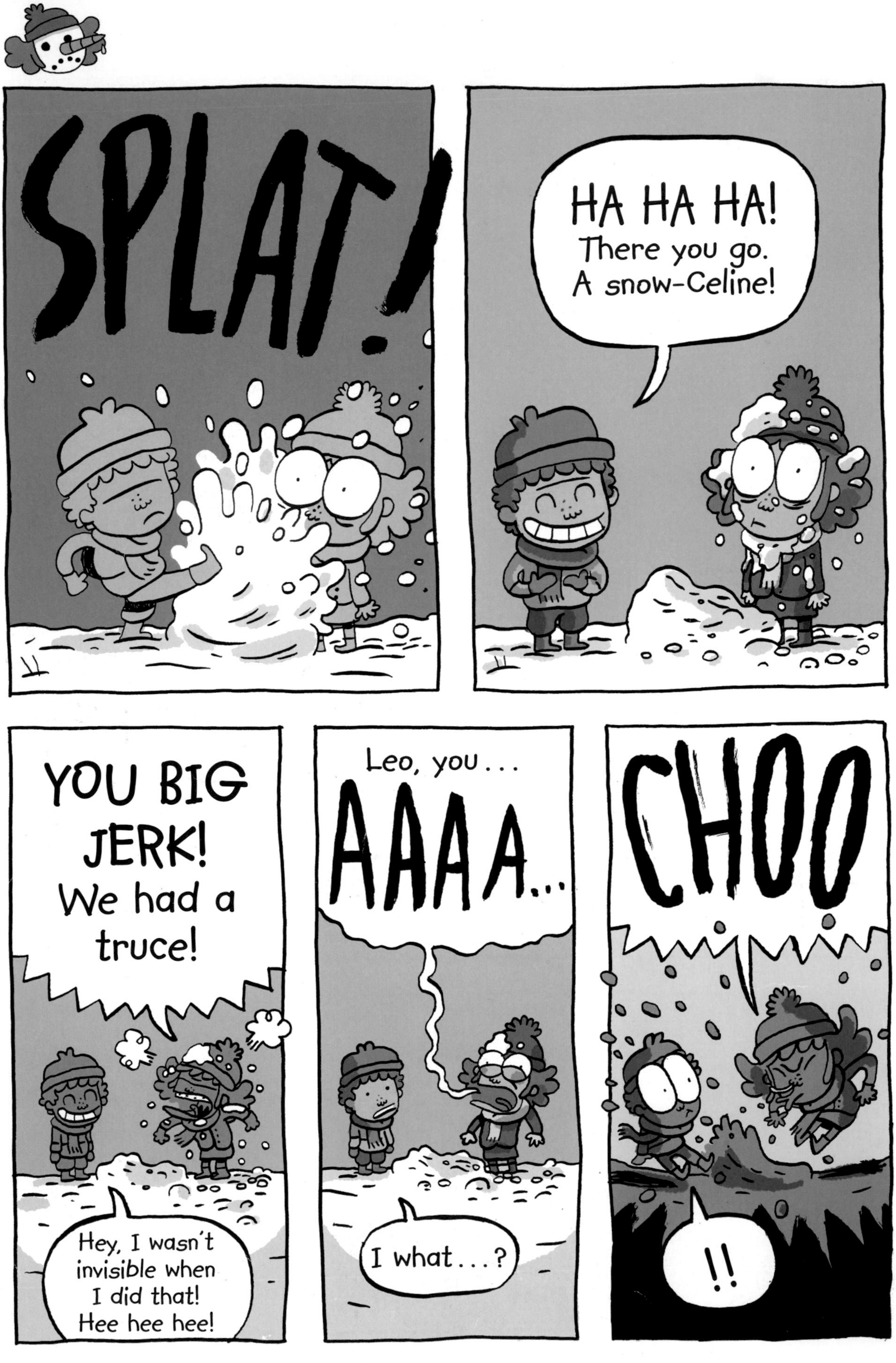
SPLAT!
HA HA HA! There you go. A snow-Celine!
YOU BIG JERK! We had a truce!
Hey, I wasn't invisible when I did that! Hee hee hee!
Leo, you . . .
AAAA...
I what . . . ?
CHOO
!!

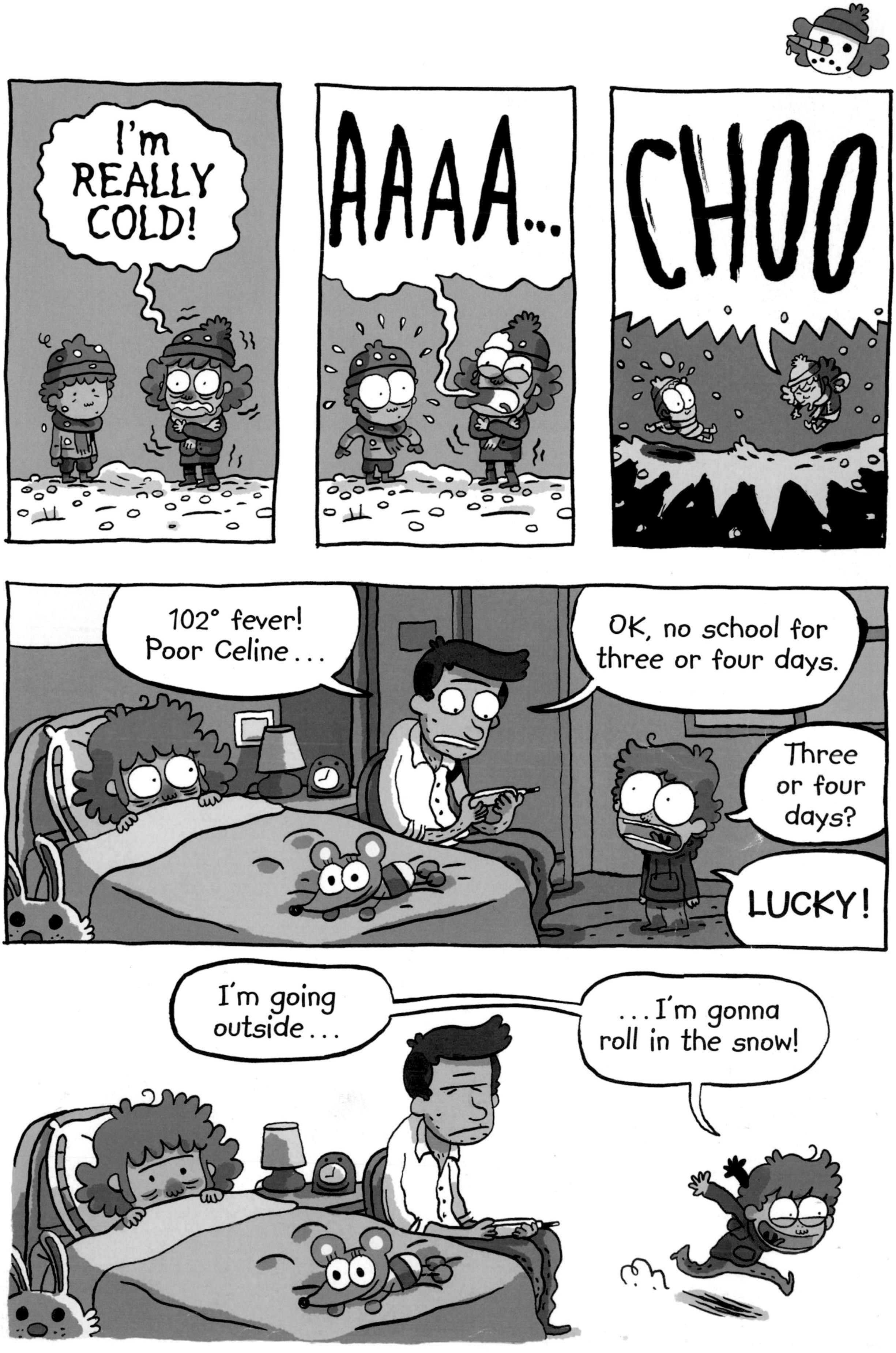
I'm REALLY COLD!
AAAA...
CHOO
102° fever! Poor Celine...
OK, no school for three or four days.
Three or four days?
LUCKY!
I'm going outside...
...I'm gonna roll in the snow!

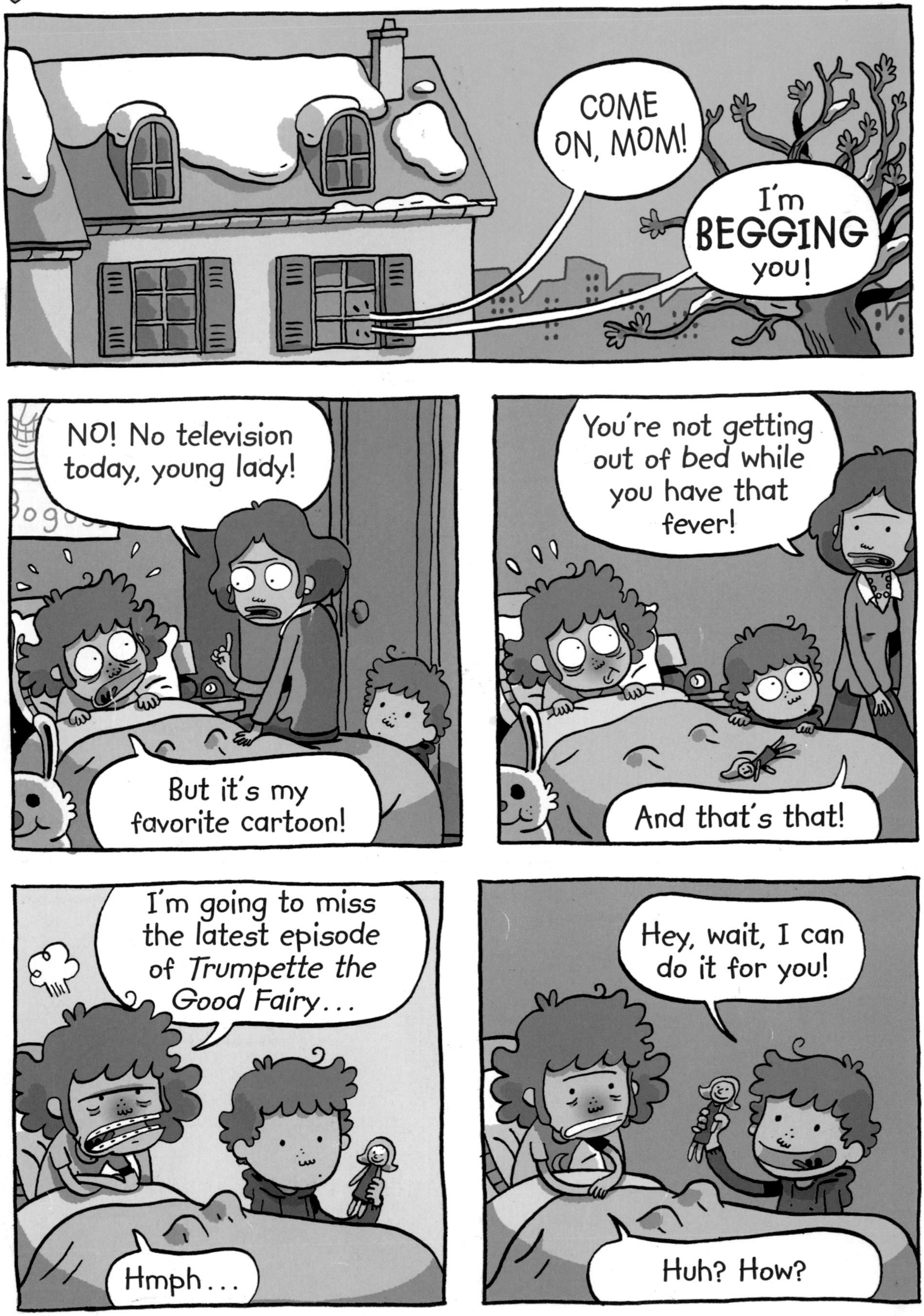
COME ON, MOM!
I'm BEGGING you!
NO! No television today, young lady!
But it's my favorite cartoon!
You're not getting out of bed while you have that fever!
And that's that!
I'm going to miss the latest episode of *Trumpette the Good Fairy*...
Hmph...
Hey, wait, I can do it for you!
Huh? How?

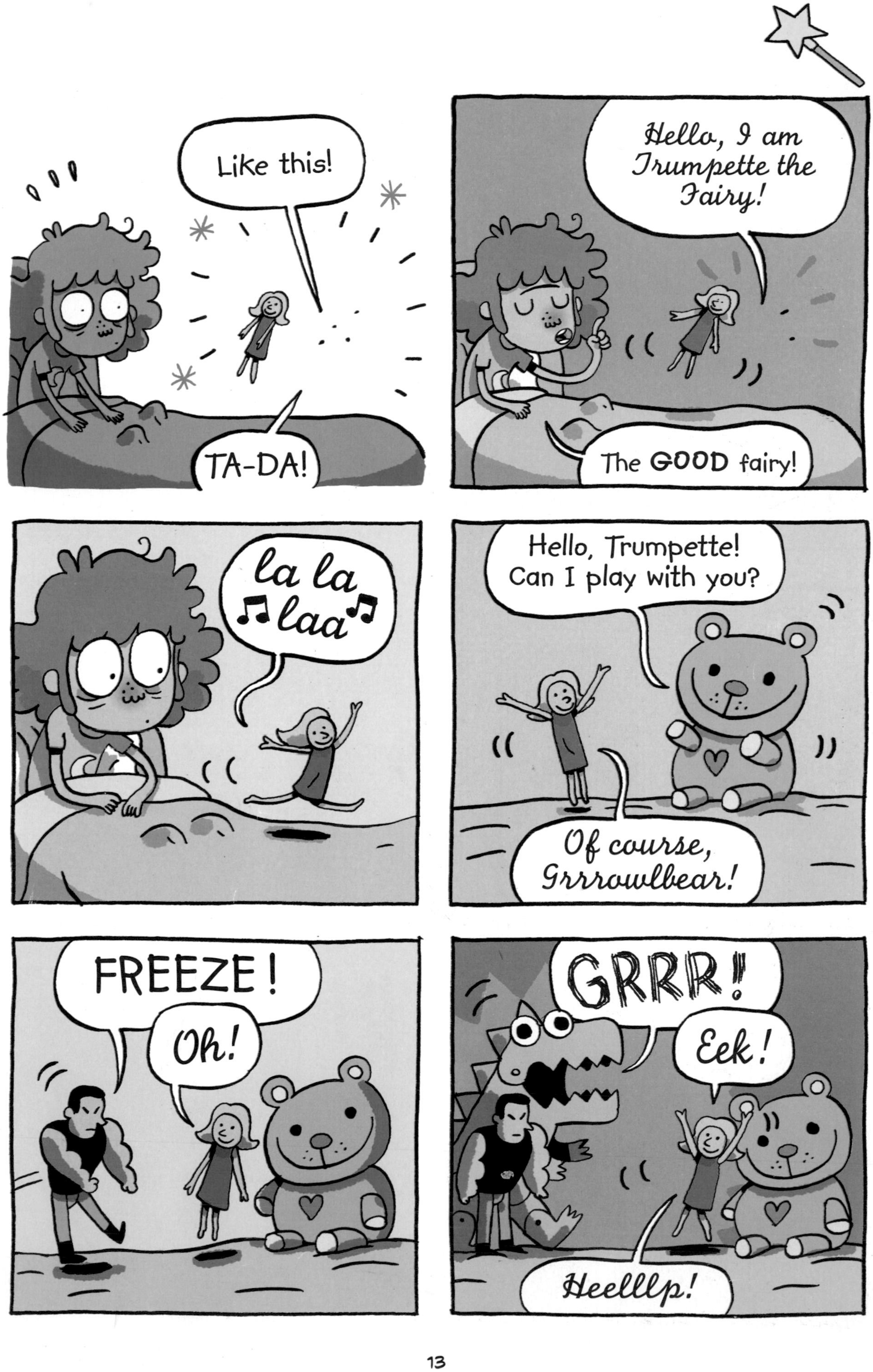
Like this!
TA-DA!
Hello, I am Trumpette the Fairy!
The GOOD fairy!
la la laa
Hello, Trumpette! Can I play with you?
Of course, Grrrowlbear!
FREEZE!
Oh!
GRRR!
Eek!
Heelllp!

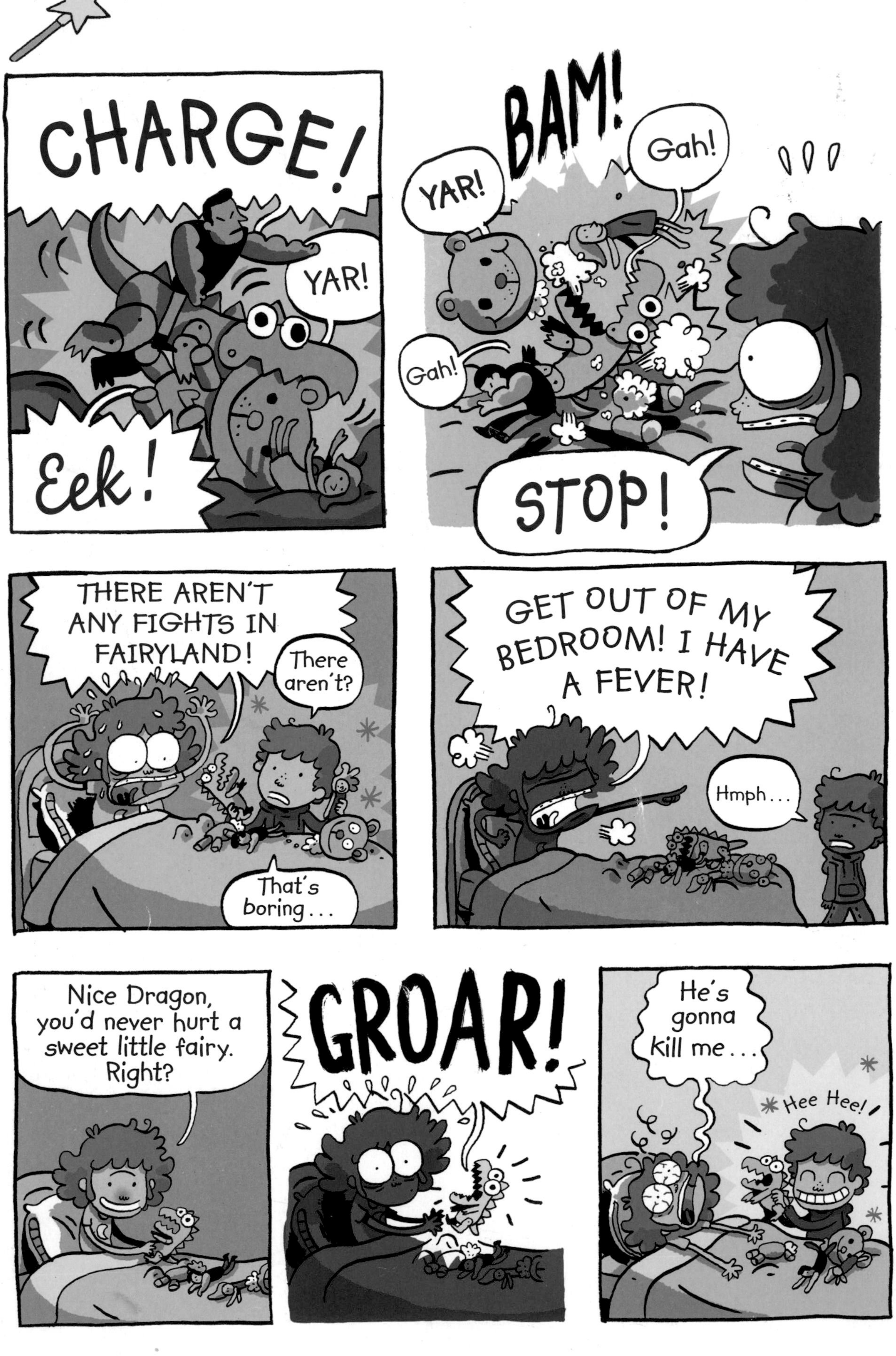
CHARGE!
YAR!
Eek!
BAM!
YAR!
Gah!
Gah!
STOP!
THERE AREN'T ANY FIGHTS IN FAIRYLAND!
There aren't?
That's boring...
GET OUT OF MY BEDROOM! I HAVE A FEVER!
Hmph...
Nice Dragon, you'd never hurt a sweet little fairy. Right?
GROAR!
He's gonna kill me...
Hee Hee!

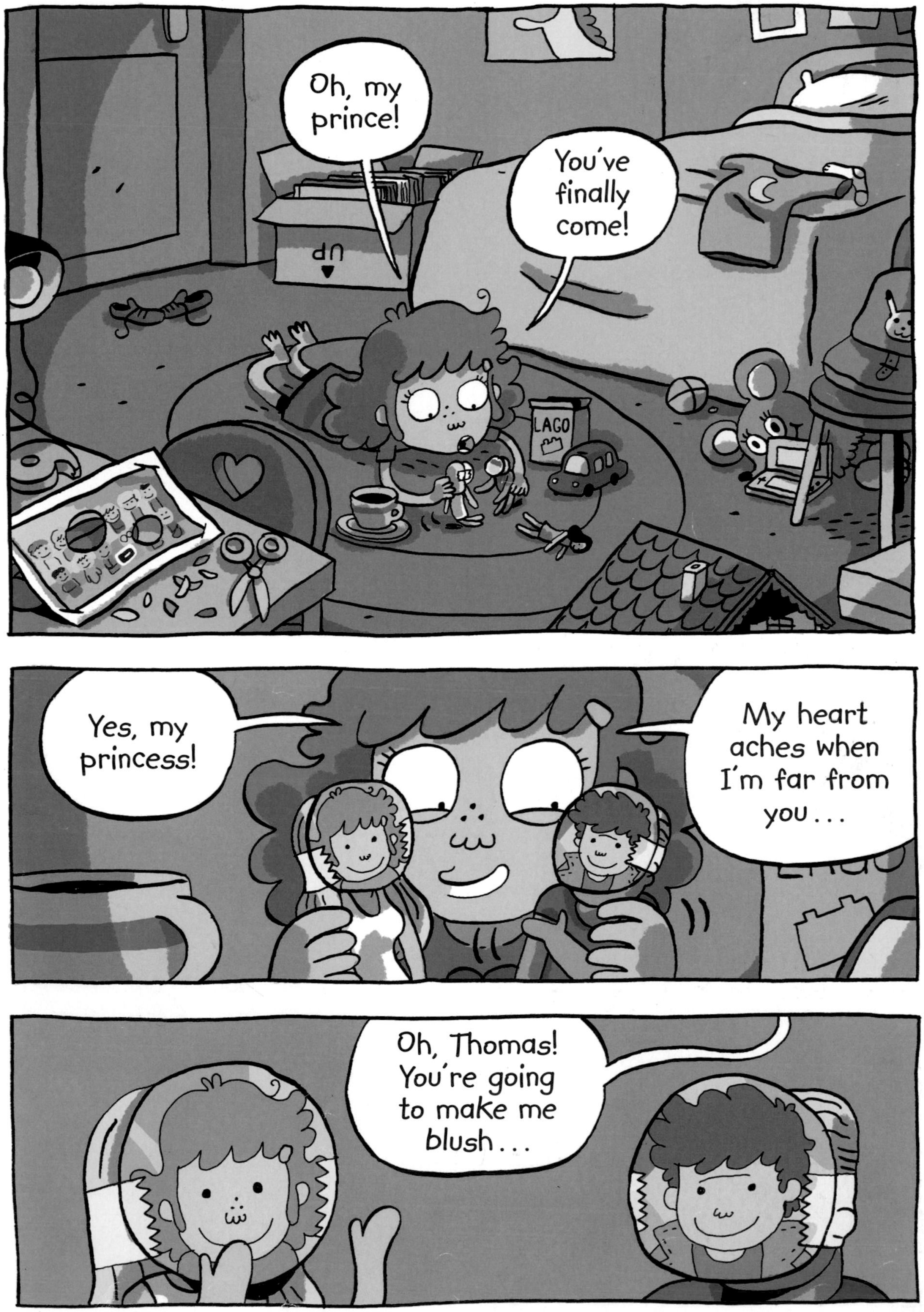
Oh, my prince!
You've finally come!
LAGO
UP
Yes, my princess!
My heart aches when I'm far from you...
Oh, Thomas! You're going to make me blush...

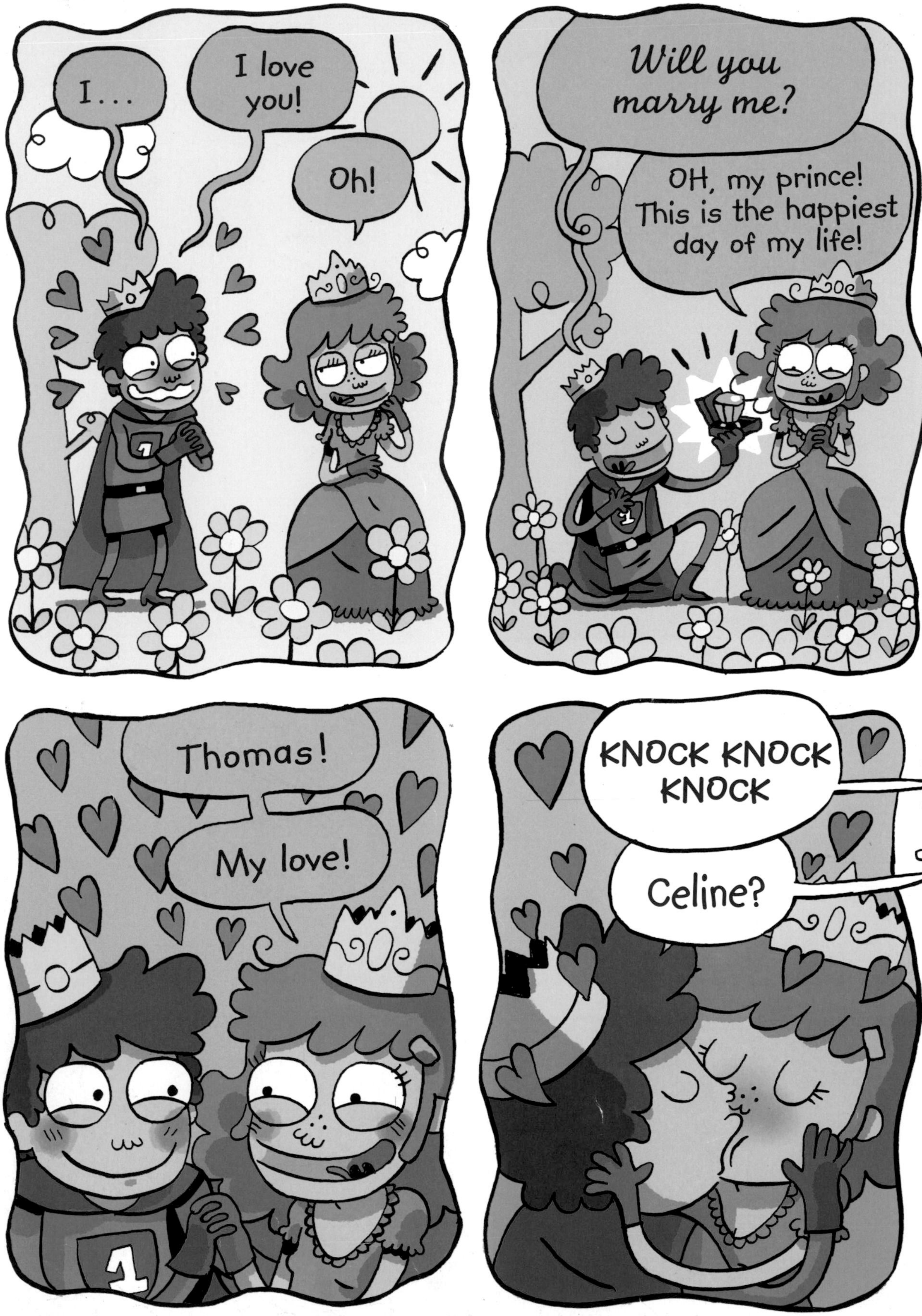
I...
I love you!
Oh!
Will you marry me?
OH, my prince! This is the happiest day of my life!
Thomas!
My love!
KNOCK KNOCK KNOCK
Celine?

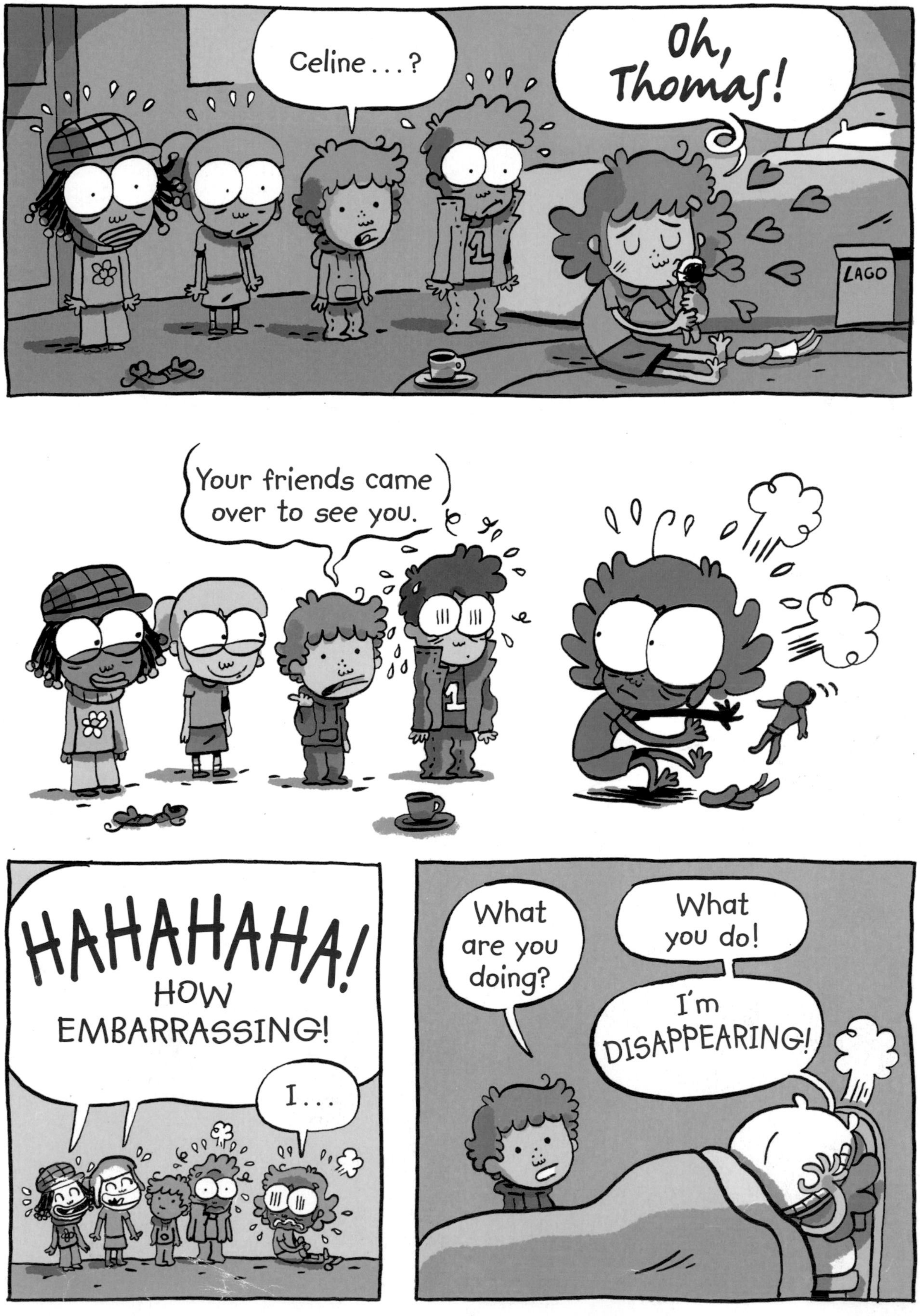

Celine . . . ?
Oh, Thomas!
LAGO
Your friends came over to see you.
HAHAHAHA! HOW EMBARRASSING!
I . . .
What are you doing?
What you do!
I'm DISAPPEARING!

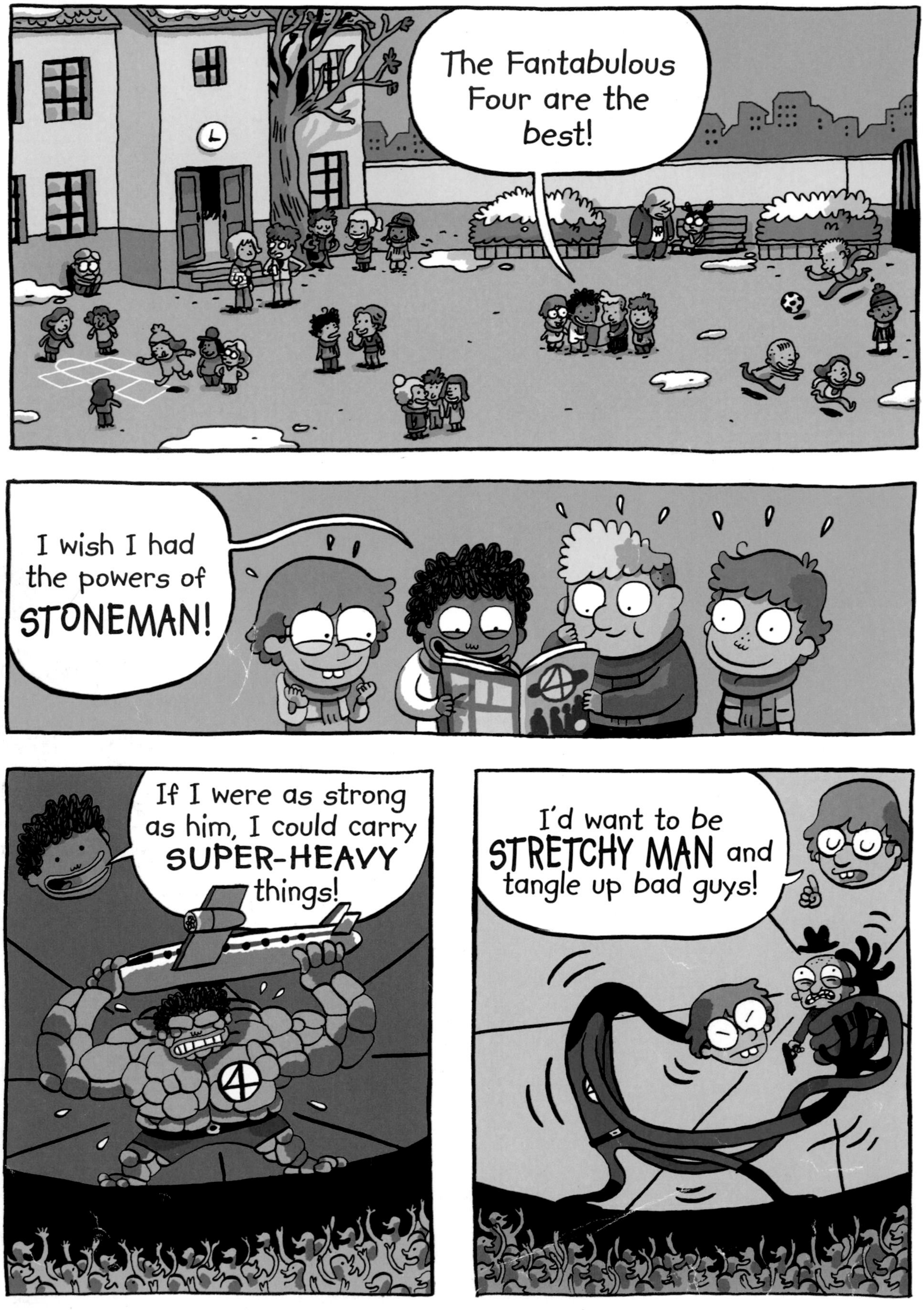
The Fantabulous Four are the best!
I wish I had the powers of STONEMAN!
If I were as strong as him, I could carry SUPER-HEAVY things!
I'd want to be STRETCHY MAN and tangle up bad guys!

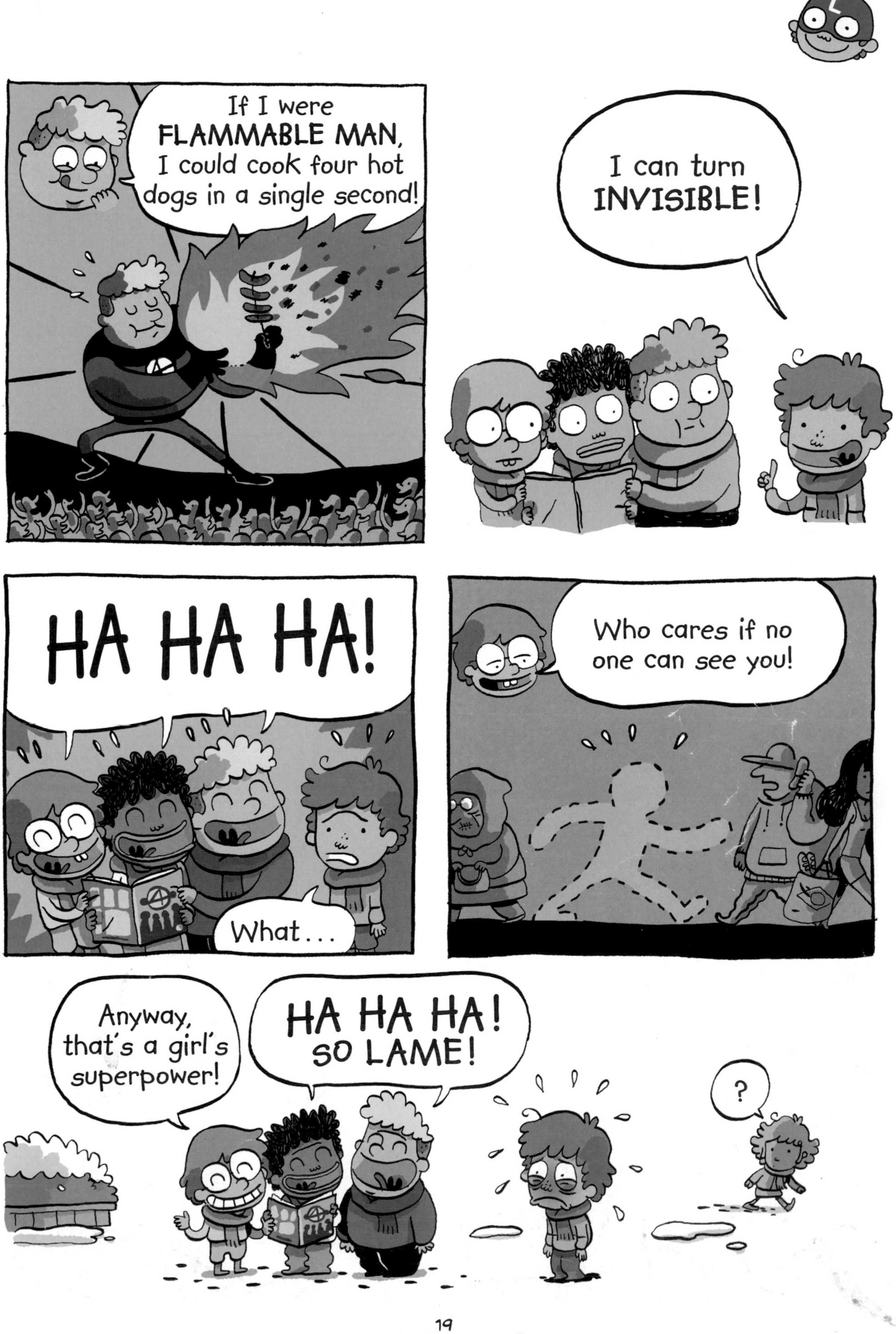
If I were FLAMMABLE MAN, I could cook four hot dogs in a single second!
I can turn INVISIBLE!
HA HA HA!
What...
Who cares if no one can see you!
Anyway, that's a girl's superpower!
HA HA HA! SO LAME!
?

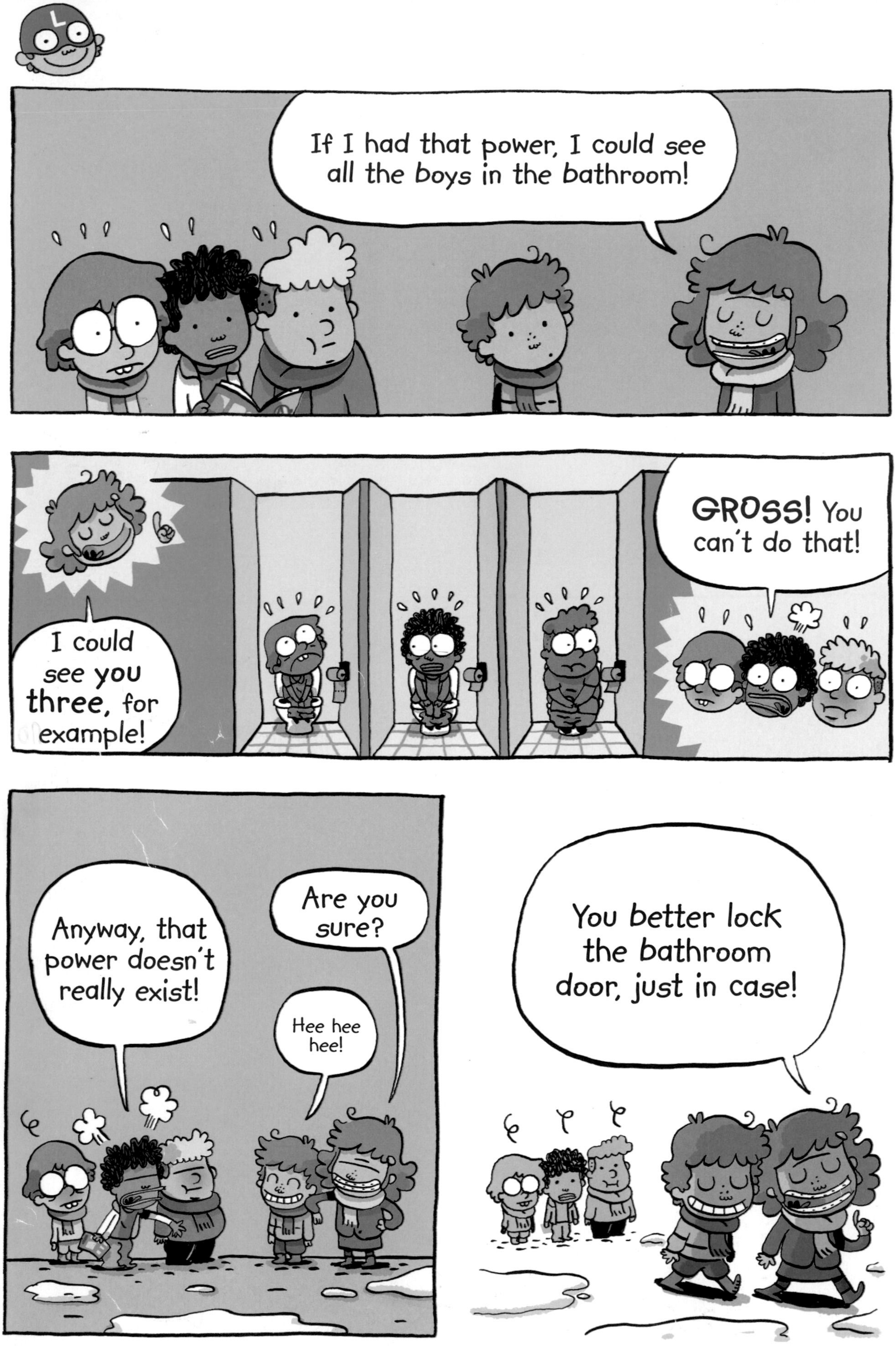
If I had that power, I could see all the boys in the bathroom!
I could see you three, for example!
GROSS! You can't do that!
Anyway, that power doesn't really exist!
Are you sure?
Hee hee hee!
You better lock the bathroom door, just in case!

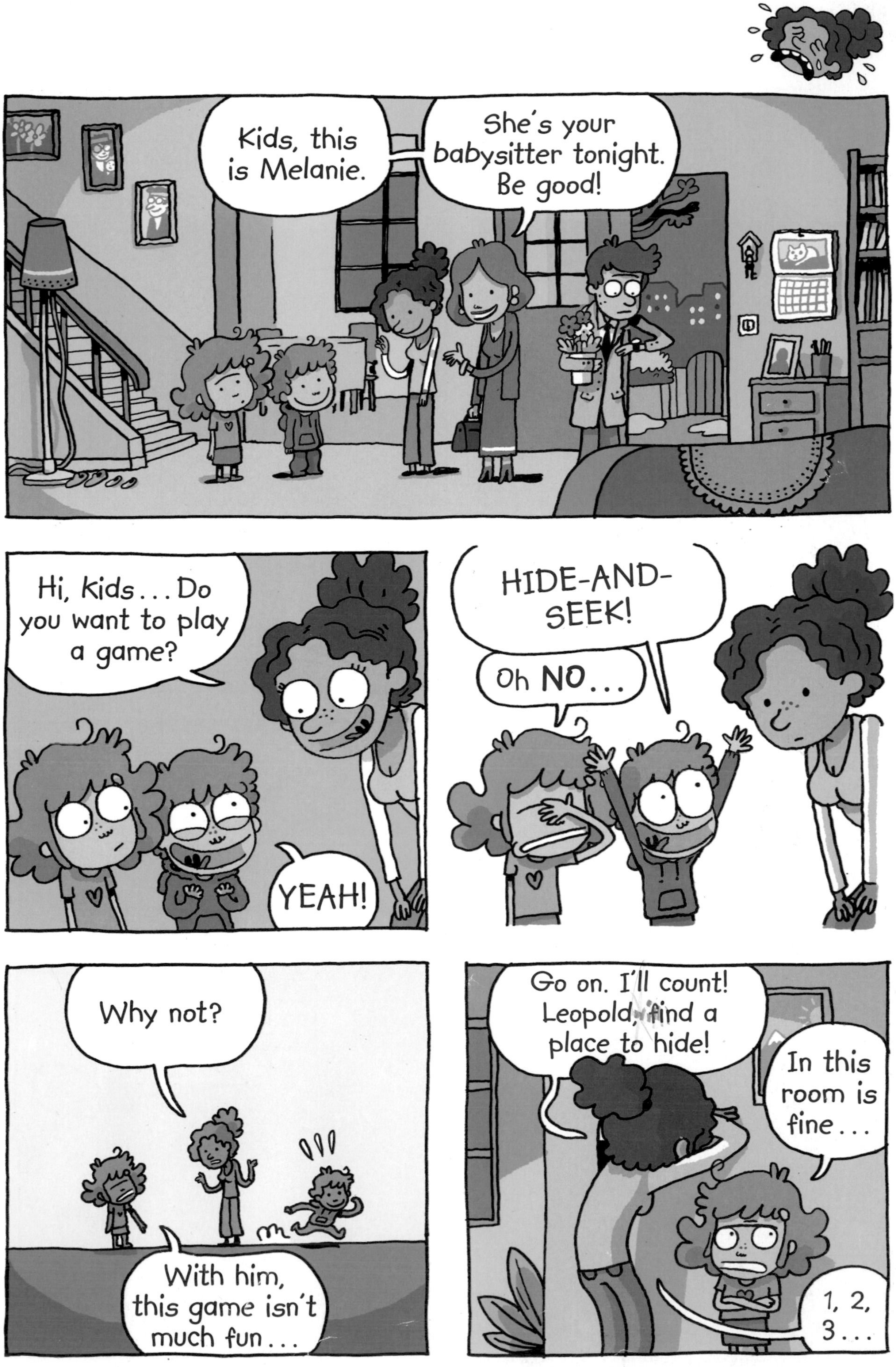
Kids, this is Melanie.
She's your babysitter tonight. Be good!
Hi, kids . . . Do you want to play a game?
YEAH!
HIDE-AND-SEEK!
Oh NO . . .
Why not?
With him, this game isn't much fun . . .
Go on. I'll count! Leopold, find a place to hide!
In this room is fine . . .
1, 2, 3 . . .

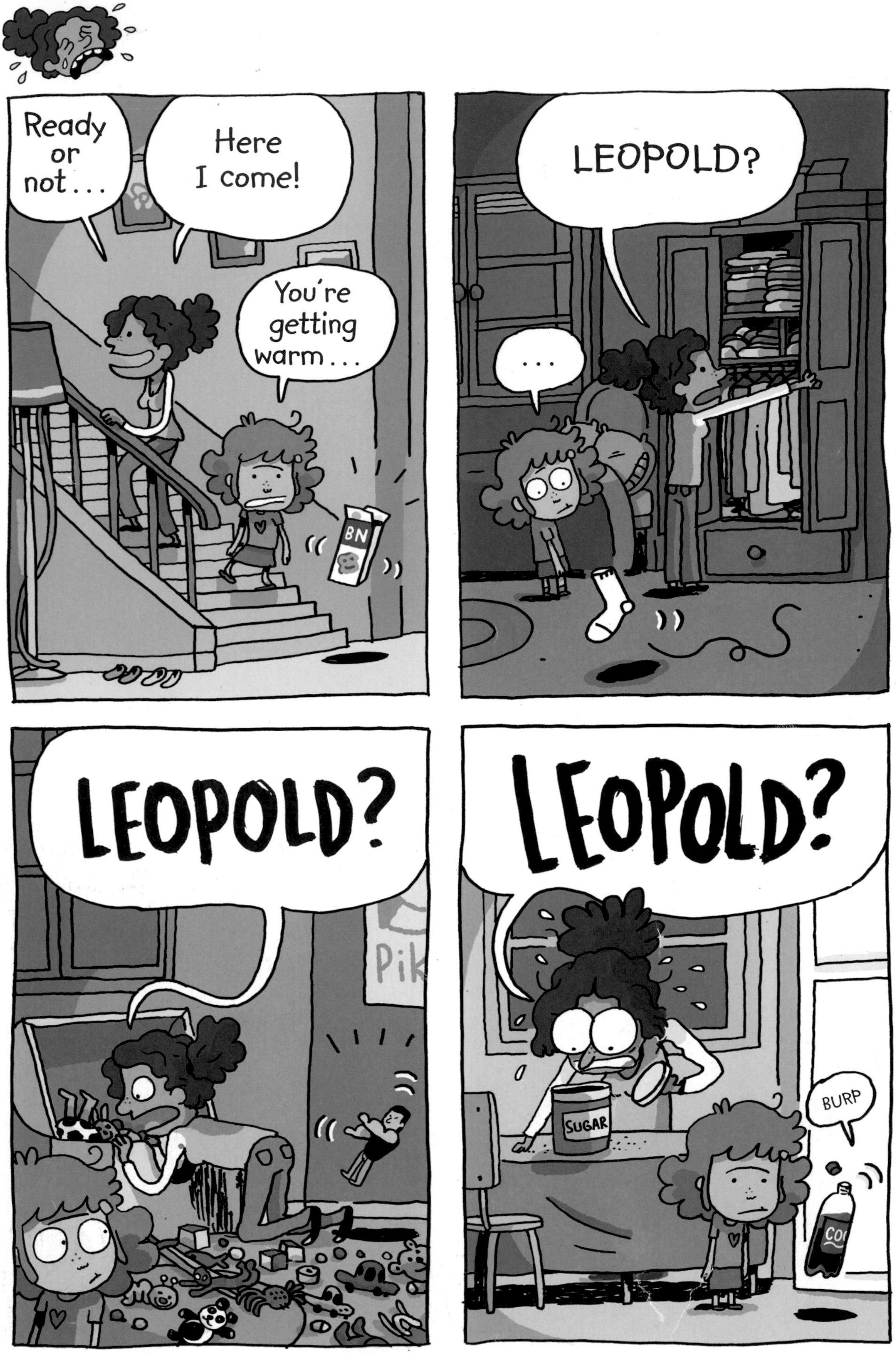
Ready or not . . .
Here I come!
You're getting warm . . .
BN
LEOPOLD?
. . .
LEOPOLD?
Pik
LEOPOLD?
SUGAR
BURP

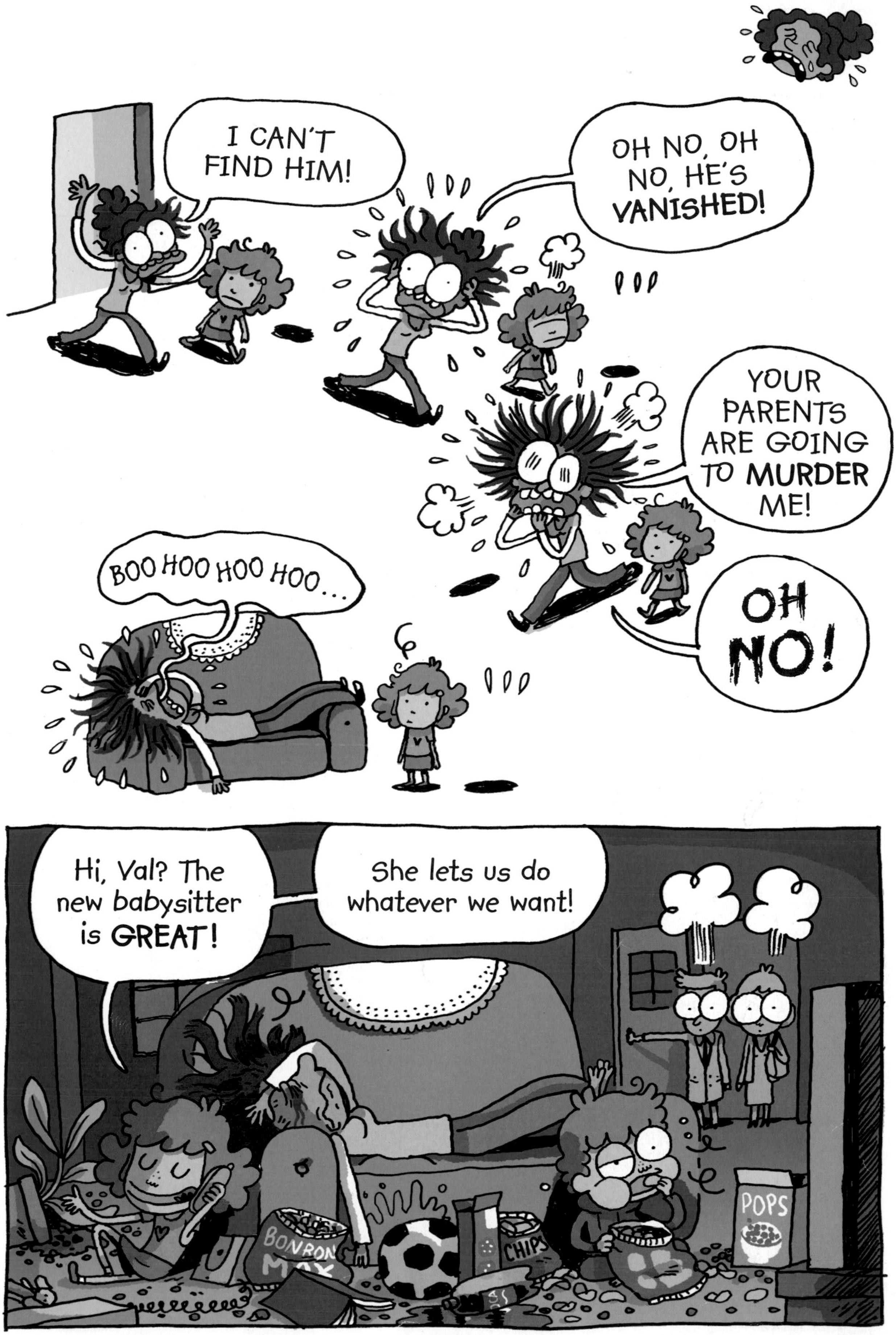
I CAN'T FIND HIM!
OH NO, OH NO, HE'S VANISHED!
YOUR PARENTS ARE GOING TO MURDER ME!
OH NO!
BOO HOO HOO HOO...
Hi, Val? The new babysitter is GREAT!
She lets us do whatever we want!
BONRON
CHIPS
POPS

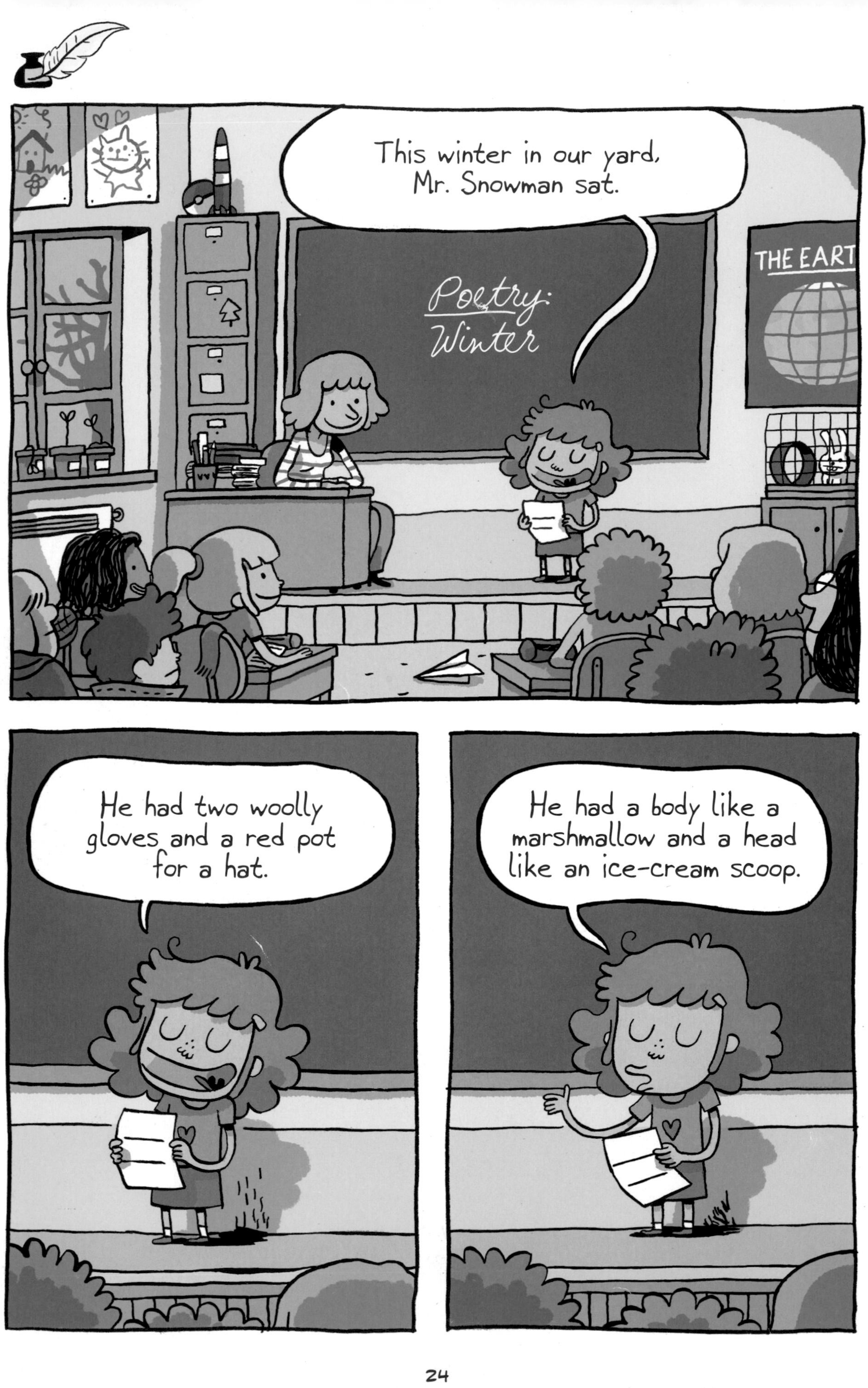
This winter in our yard, Mr. Snowman sat.
Poetry: Winter
THE EART
He had two woolly gloves and a red pot for a hat.
He had a body like a marshmallow and a head like an ice-cream scoop.

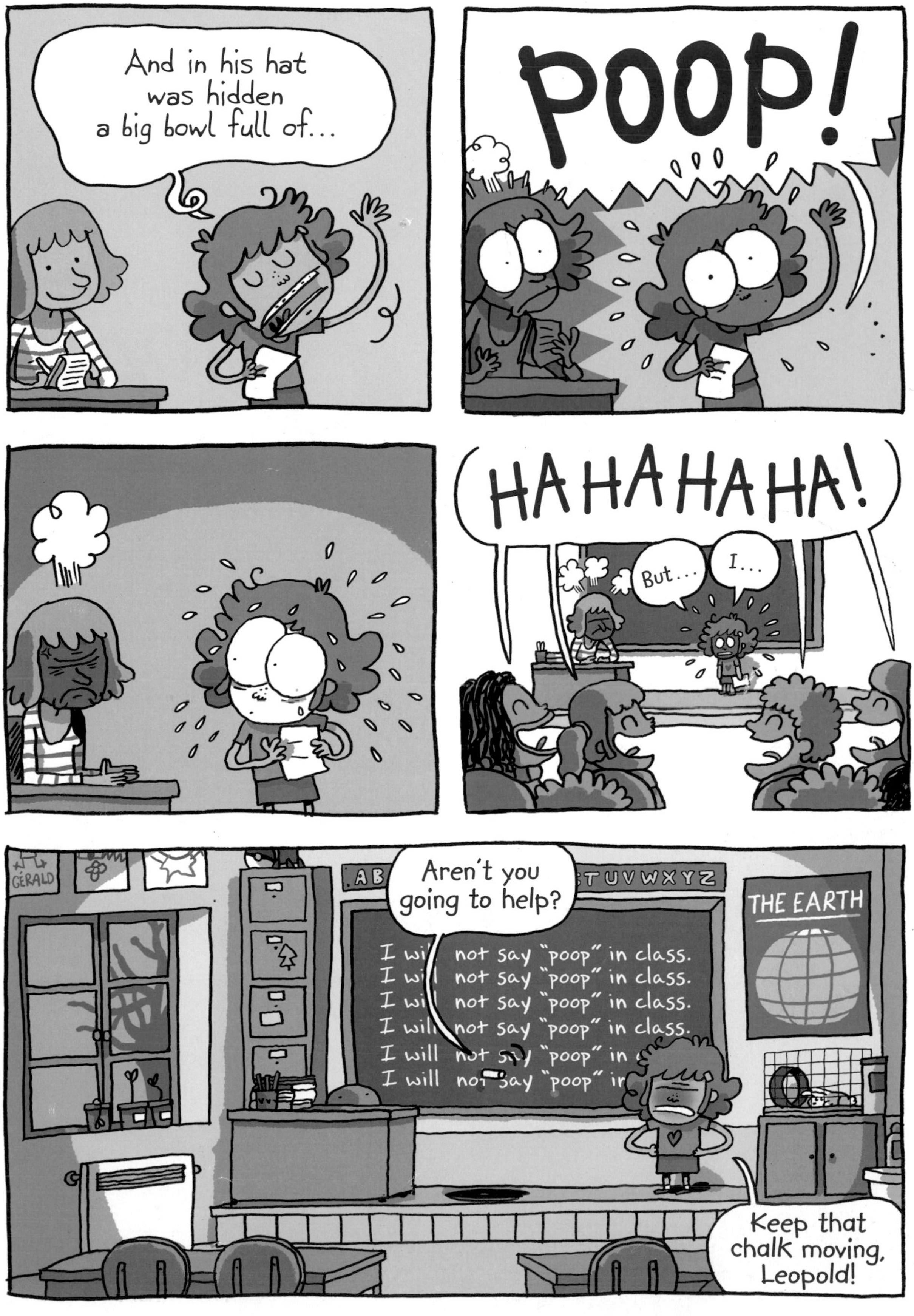
And in his hat was hidden a big bowl full of...
POOP!
HA HA HA HA HA!
But...
I...
Aren't you going to help?
THE EARTH
GERALD
I will not say "poop" in class.
I will not say "poop" in class.
I will not say "poop" in class.
I will not say "poop" in class.
I will not say "poop" in
I will not say "poop" in
Keep that chalk moving, Leopold!

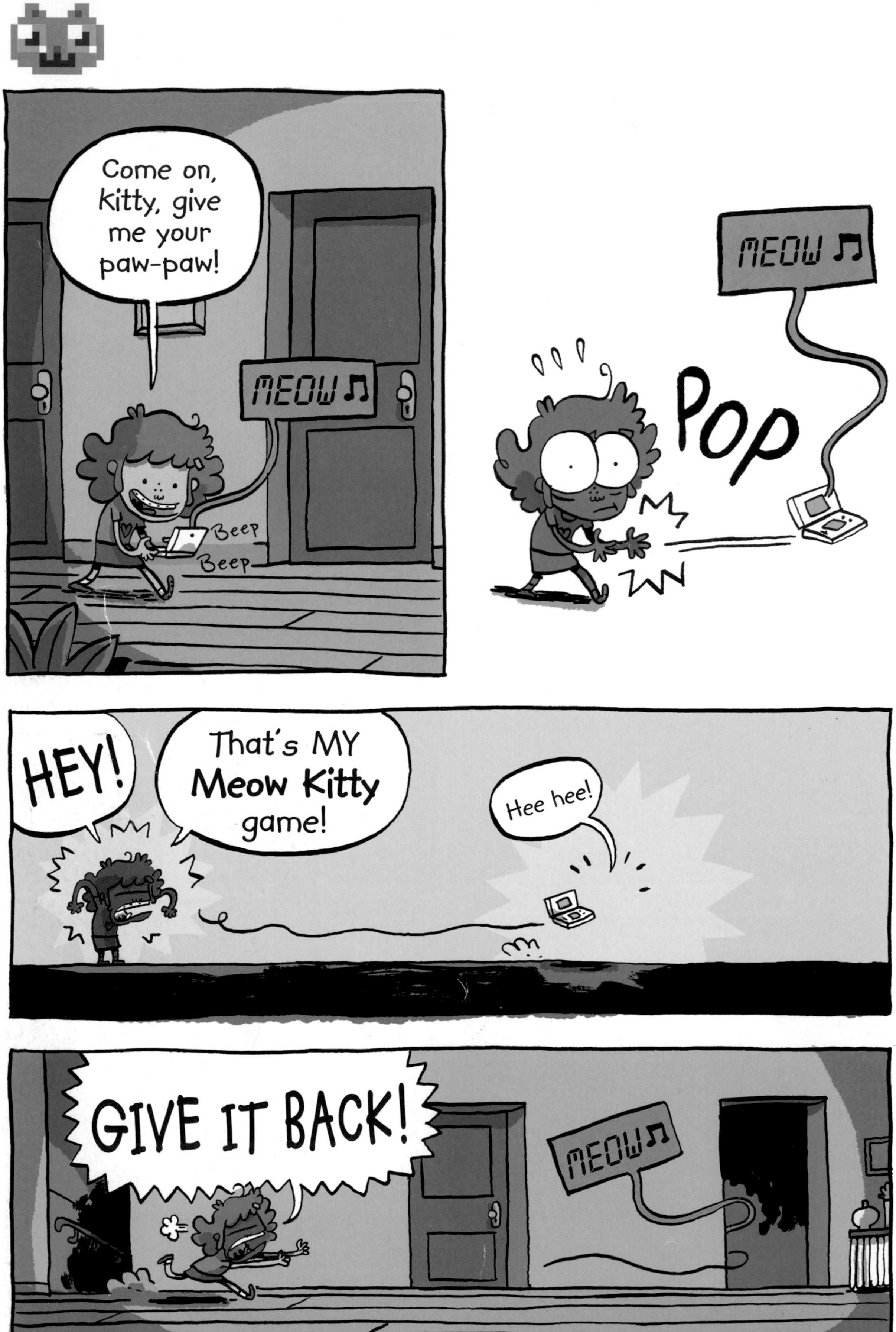
Come on, kitty, give me your paw-paw!
MEOW ♫
Beep
Beep
MEOW ♫
POP
HEY!
That's MY **Meow Kitty** game!
Hee hee!
GIVE IT BACK!
MEOW ♫

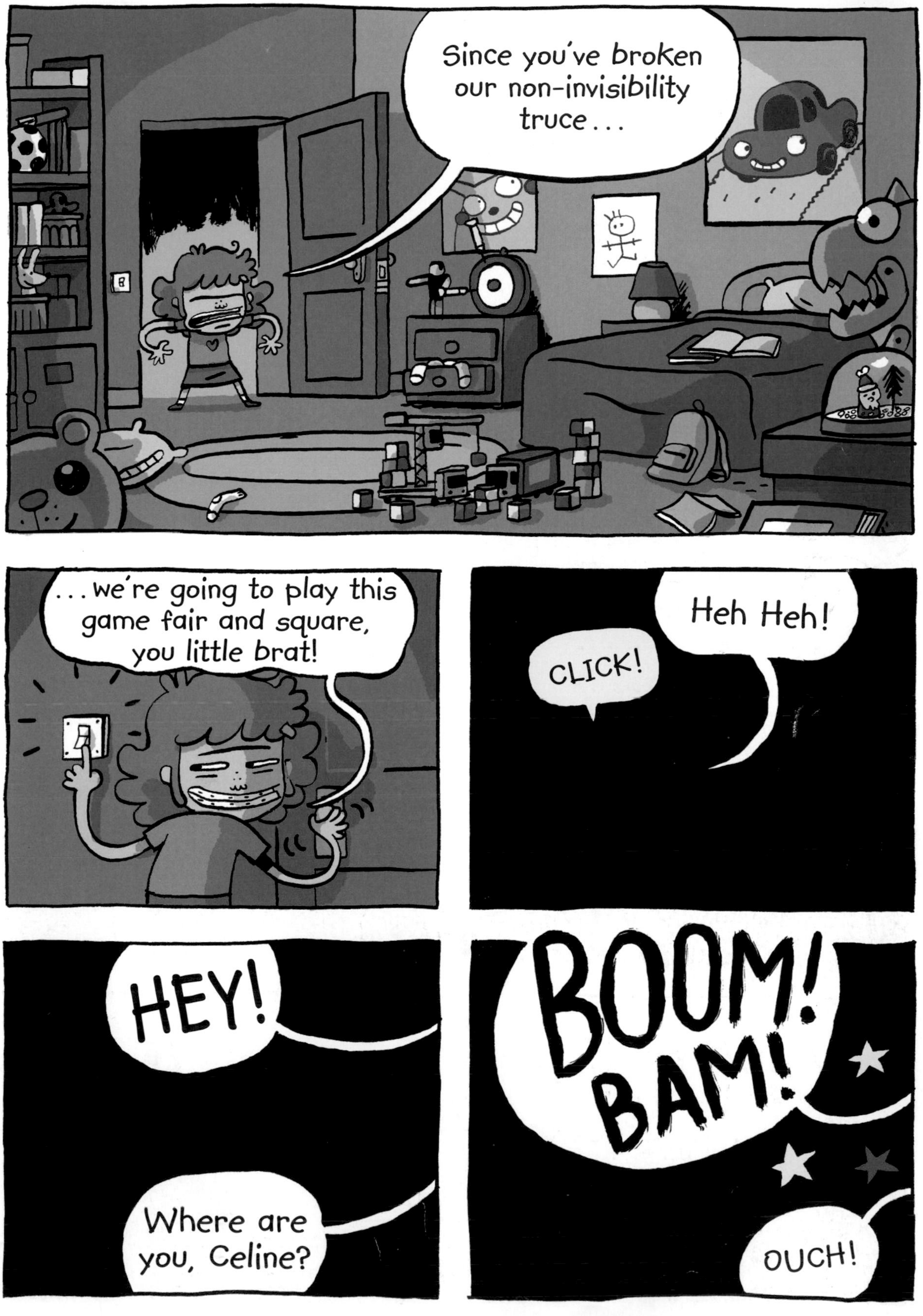
Since you've broken our non-invisibility truce . . .
. . . we're going to play this game fair and square, you little brat!
CLICK!
Heh Heh!
HEY!
Where are you, Celine?
BOOM! BAM!
OUCH!

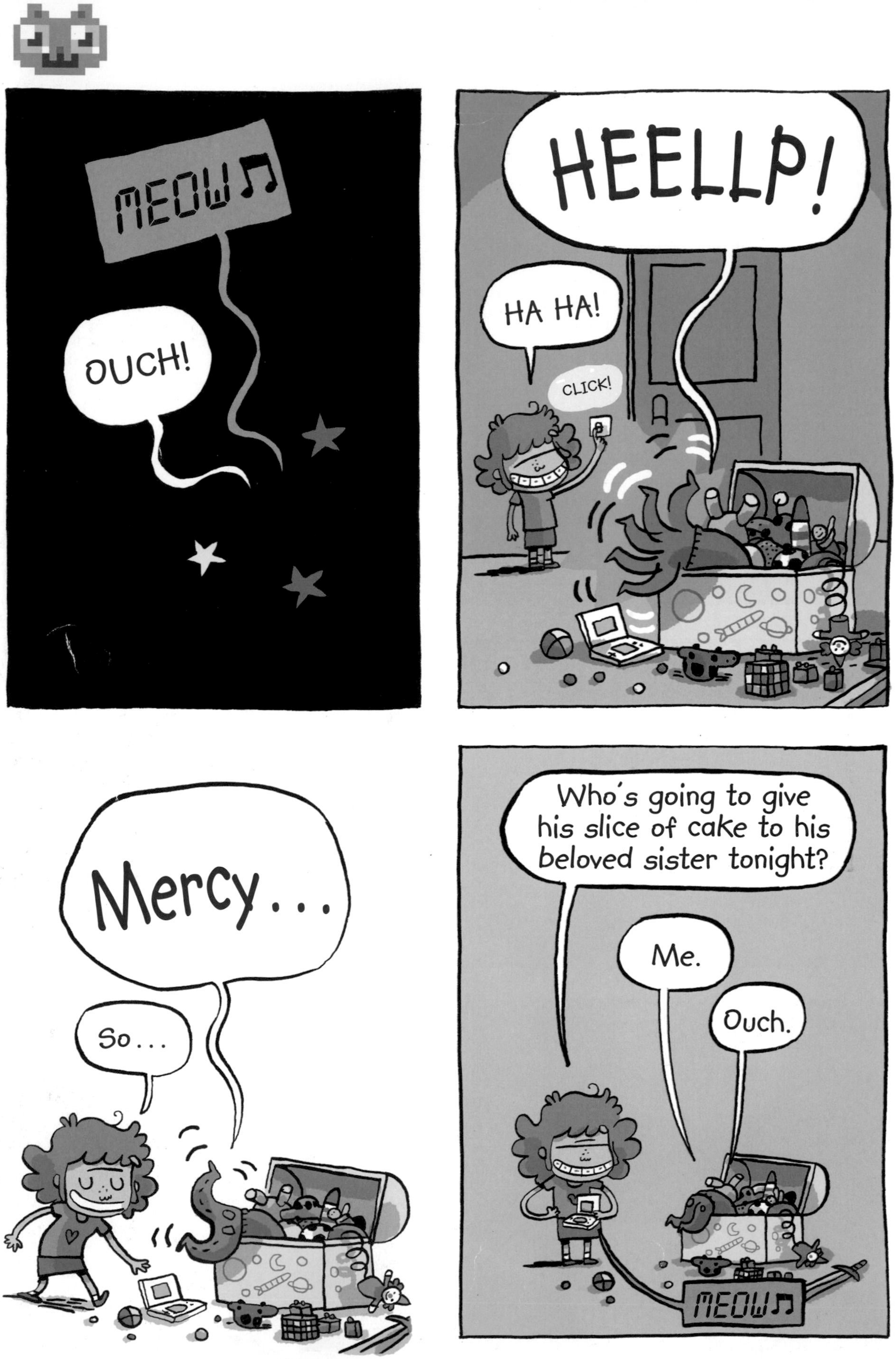
MEOW♫
OUCH!
HEELLP!
HA HA!
CLICK!
Mercy...
So...
Who's going to give his slice of cake to his beloved sister tonight?
Me.
Ouch.
MEOW♫

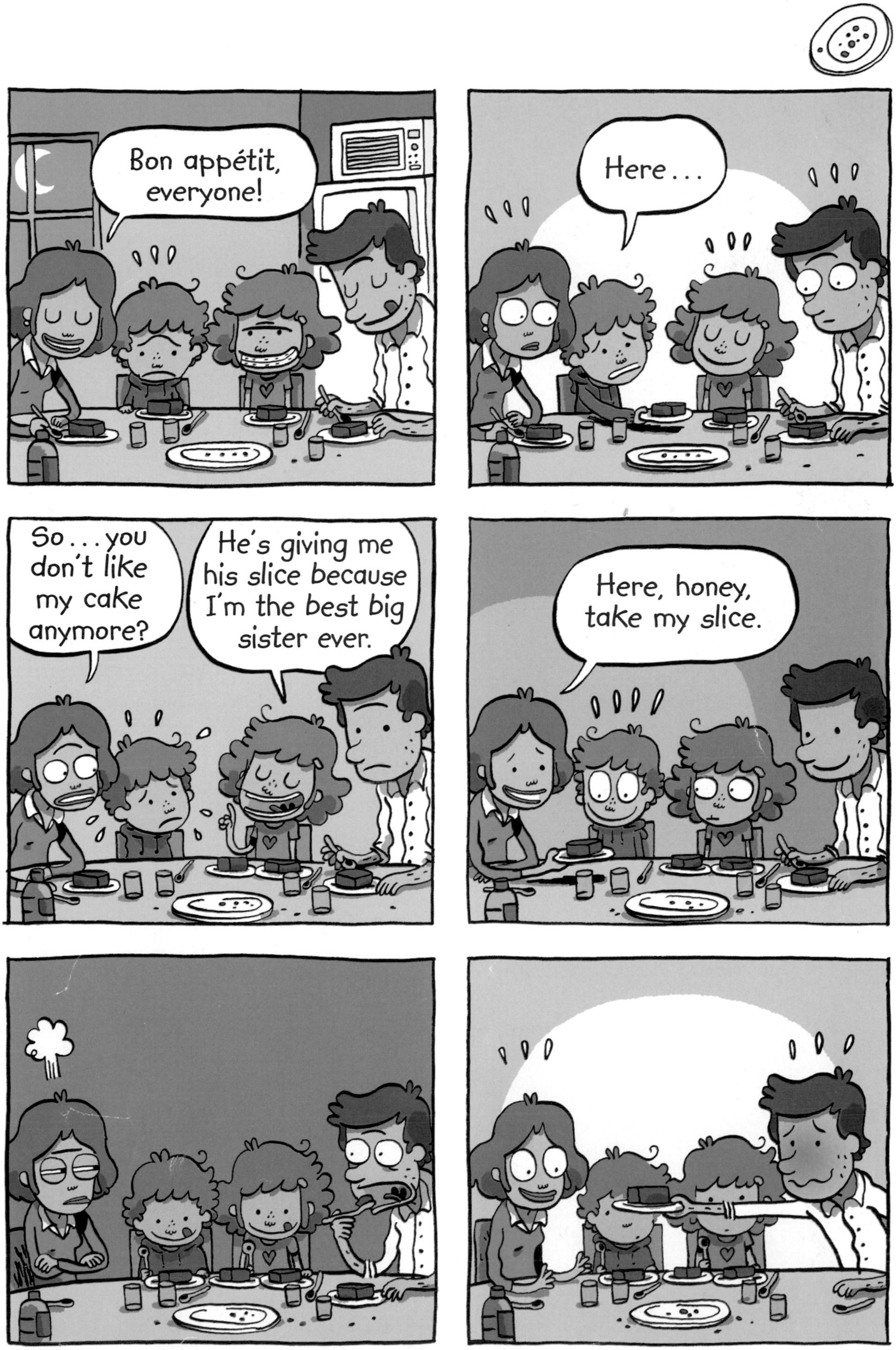
Bon appétit, everyone!
Here . . .
So . . . you don't like my cake anymore?
He's giving me his slice because I'm the best big sister ever.
Here, honey, take my slice.

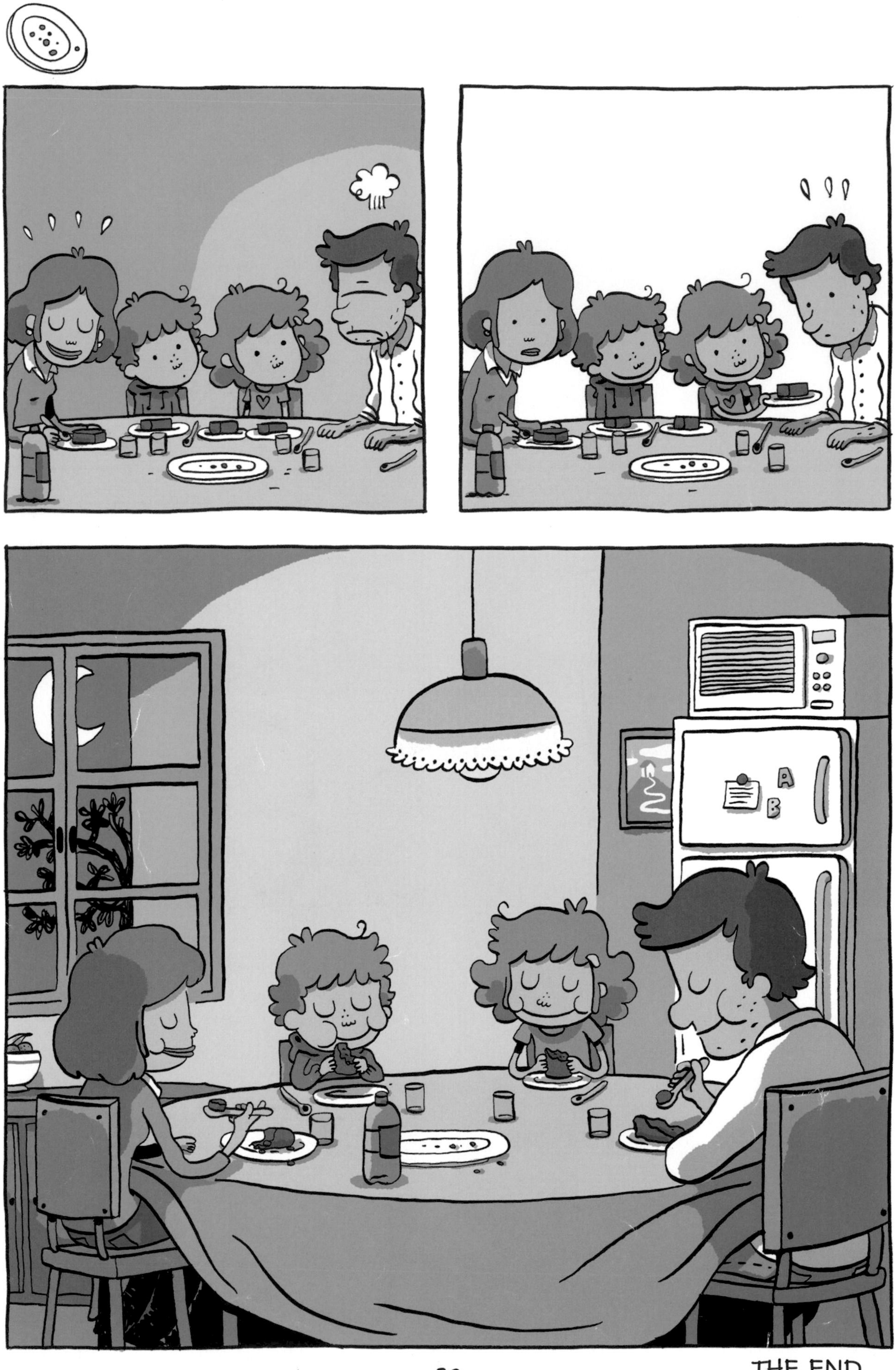
A
B

THE END

Michel-Yves Schmitt was born in Bordeaux, France, but he grew up in the city of Nantes. He studied both applied arts and fine arts before moving to Paris to become a graphic designer. During these early years, he drew cartoons for the zines *Beurk!* and *Goinfre.* Later, his work appeared mostly in professional publications, including the comic magazine *Patate Douce.* Schmitt is the author and illustrator of the slice-of-life graphic novels *Dérives, Ainsi danse*, and *Ma vie d'adulte.* He also collaborated with artist Cédric Kernel to create a Wild West comic titled *La Poire en deux.* He then spent three years working as an artist on the Geronimo Stilton animated series. Most recently, he teamed up with Vincent Caut to create Où es-tu Léopold? (the French title for **Where's Leopold?** series), which received the Prize for School Comic at the Angoulême International Comics Festival in 2012.

Vincent Caut was born in Melun, a suburb of Paris. At the age of thirteen, he discovered webcomics and decided to make his own. Eight years later, he was awarded the Grand Prize for Promising Young Talent and the Revelation Second Prize at the Angoulême International Comics Festival. He then wrote and drew his first book, *Le Trésor de l'Île Mokoko*. His other solo works include *Quelle Tête en l'Air!*, *Les Aventures de la Fin du Monde*, and *Soit dit en passant, journal d'un étudiant*. He teamed up with Sophie Lamoureux to create a graphic novel about the Plains Indians called *Les Indiens d'Amérique à petits pas*. It was around this time that he collaborated with Michel-Yves Schmitt to create **Where's Leopold?**

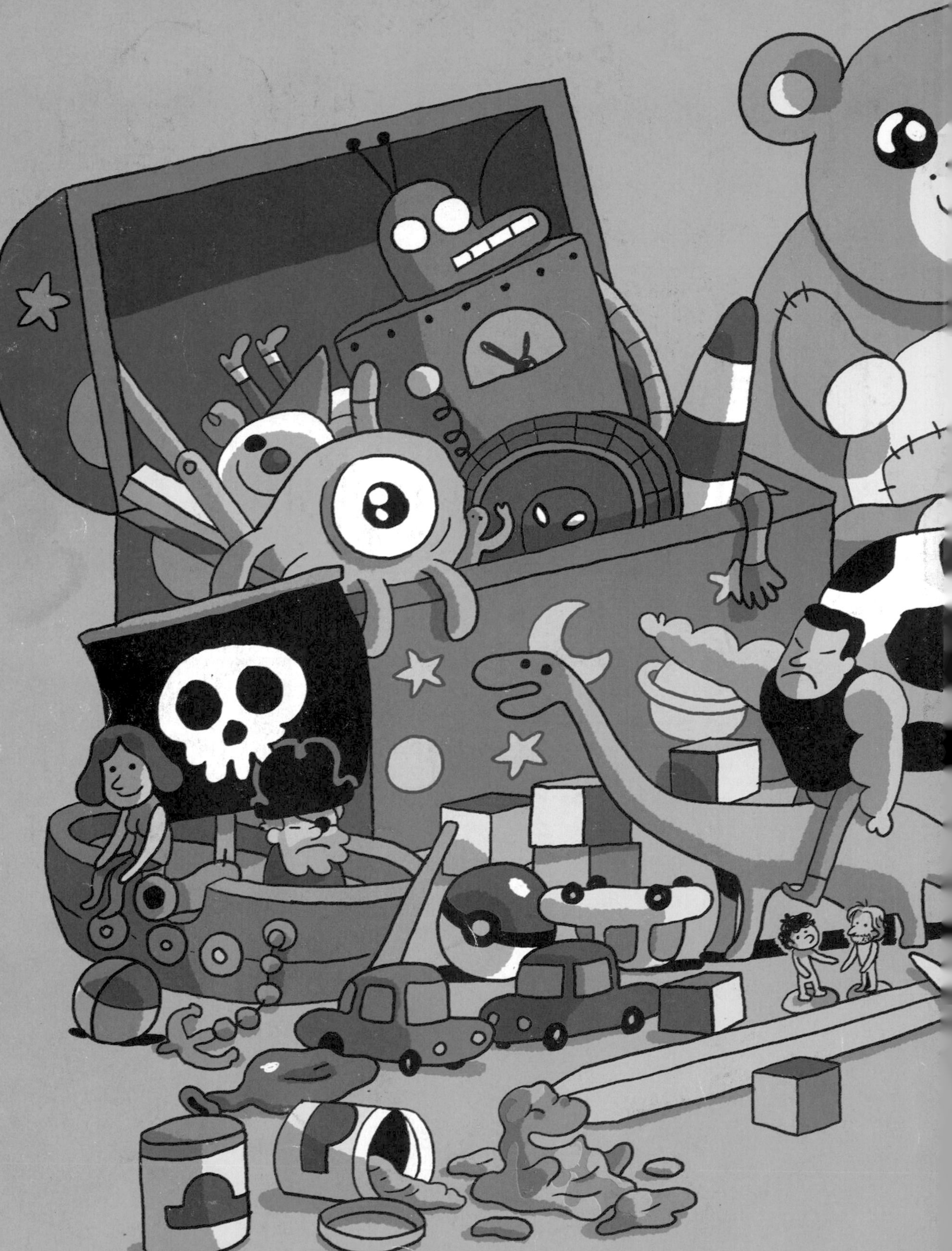